T0167979

THE BOOK OF VENICE

THE BOOK OF VENICE

EDITED BY ORSOLA CASAGRANDE

Translated by Orsola Casagrande
& Caterina Dell'Olivo

Part of Comma's 'Reading the City' series

First published in Great Britain by Comma Press, 2021
www.commapress.co.uk

Copyright © remains with the authors, translators and Comma Press, 2021.
All rights reserved.

The moral rights of the contributors to be identified as the authors and translators
of this Work have been asserted in accordance with the Copyright Designs
and Patents Act 1988.

'Carmen' by Elisabetta Baldisserotto was the Winner of the Critics' Award at
Pordenonelegge 2002, and was first published in *2019 Un Anno di Storie,* (CLEUP, ·
Padova, 2018). 'Laguna' ('Lagoon') by Roberto Ferrucci was first published in
Venezia è laguna (Venice is lagoon, Helvetia Editrice, 2019). 'Perché comincio dalla
fine' ('Why I Begin at the End') by Ginevra Lamberti was first published in Italy by
Marsilio Editori in 2019. Her story is published in agreement with MalaTesta
Literary Agency, Milan. 'Le Condizioni Atmosferiche' (Atmospheric Conditions) by
Enrico Palandri previously published in *Le Condizioni Atmosferiche,* (Bonaparte,
2020). All the other stories were written especially for this anthology, and published
here for the first time.

The stories in this anthology are entirely works of fiction. The names, characters and
incidents portrayed in them are entirely the work of the authors' imagination. Any
resemblance to actual persons, living or dead, events, organisations or localities, is
entirely coincidental. Any characters that appear, or claim to be based on real ones are
intended to be entirely fictional. The opinions of the authors and the editors are not
those of the publisher.

A CIP catalogue record of this book is available from the British Library.

ISBN: 1910974099
ISBN-13: 9781910974094

The publisher gratefully acknowledges the support of Arts Council England.

Supported using public funding by
**ARTS COUNCIL
ENGLAND**

Contents

CONTENTS

Introduction

'Memory's images, once they are fixed in words, are erased,'
Polo said. 'Perhaps I am afraid of losing Venice all at once, if
I speak of it, or perhaps, speaking of other cities, I have
already lost it, little by little.'

Italo Calvino, Invisible Cities

'HOPELESSLY BEAUTIFUL' AND 'THE most enchanted thing on earth' are two plaudits the American author Truman Capote used to describe Venice when he visited the city in 1948.[1] Such superlatives have no doubt been heaped on the city throughout her long history, and for good reason, given her uniqueness and the way that uniqueness has been reiterated and perpetuated through time by her own apparent stasis, her seeming inability to change or move with the times.

And yet, Venice *has* changed a lot through the centuries and keeps changing. Founded in the fifth century AD, after the fall of the Roman Empire, she is the result of Germanic and Hun invaders forcing large numbers of mainlanders to flee and seek refuge in the islands of the lagoon, which, until then, had only been inhabited by fishermen and salt collectors. These refugee-settlers showed miraculous ingenuity, draining areas of the lagoon by digging canals and shoring up the banks. The use of long wooden piles (around 60 feet long), driven vertically through the soft lagoon silt into the hard clay beneath, proved to be perhaps their greatest innovation: providing foundations sturdy enough to build upon. And build they did, spectacularly so, creating the Venice we know today: an archipelago of 118 islands, criss-crossed by 177 canals, and connected together again by some 400 bridges.

The history of Venice's transformation is told in her street and canal names, as seen written on the white, painted rectangles on their walls called nizioleti – literally, little sheets. You can deduce a lot about the city just by reading the nizioleti. You can see which canals (rio) were later filled with earth and transformed into just streets (rio terà), or which trades took place in which street, square or neighbourhood (Calegheri – shoemakers; Orefici – jewellers). The nizioleti also tell anecdotes, in some cases even bloody ones, like the Calle dei Assassini (Assassins Street), which earned its name from the many murders committed there (being an ideal place for robberies as a small, secluded alley often taken by wealthy people not wanting to be seen heading for the brothels in nearby Calle della Mandola).

The nizioleti also reflect the many different communities that began living in Venice during her eleven centuries as a Republic, from 697 to 1797 (places like Ponte dei Greci, Campo dei Mori, Salizada del Fontego dei Turchi, Calle dei Albanesi, Calle dei Armeni, and so on). Known as La Serenissima ('the Most Serene Republic'), Venice mastered many of the world's key trade routes during this era, acting as an autonomous city-state and maritime Republic that brought much of the world back to her own shores. Marco Polo most famously left a detailed account of his journeys to the East, along the Silk Road, but there were other fascinating writers, historians and poets living and working in Venice throughout the Republic until that period in her history came to an abrupt end on 12 May 1797 with the invasion of Napoleon Bonaparte. For the next half-century, Venice would bounce back and forth between Austrian rule (from 1798-1805) to being part of Napoleon's 'Kingdom of Italy'[2] (1805-1814), then back to Austrian rule, even enjoying a brief 'revival' as an independent Republic (lasting just one year) in 1848, thanks to the revolutionary leader Daniele Manin. Eventually, after the defeat of Austria by the Prussians in 1866, Venice was ceded to Italy properly, which had been unified in 1861.

The history of twentieth-century Venice (and especially post-World War II Venice) is the history of the battle between two opposing views of what the future of this unique city should be: those that felt her delicate balance should be protected and those that felt commercialisation (in the name of modernisation) was unstoppable. Up until the '70s, Venice managed to be a political, social and cultural laboratory, keeping its various ingredients in some sort of equilibrium: the unique daily struggle of living in a place where everything has to be done by boat or foot; Venice's 'shared-with-the-world' status; her working-class heart (Porto Marghera); and her need to find a way of developing that preserved both her fragile structures and the people living there.

During this time, it was also a city of culture, often radical, experimental, innovatory, culture. Near the house that once belonged to the eighteenth-century playwright Carlo Goldoni (now a museum housing his original manuscripts), on Rio Terà dei Nomboli, there is the generic 'Murano Glass Shop' (a typical fate for so many local Venetian stores sacrificed on the altar of tourists). This was once the site of Libreria Internazionale, an anarchist bookshop, owned by the now almost century-old Silvano Gosparini, known only as 'Silvano' to his Venetian customers. The bookshop shop once hosted hundreds of meetings, talks, and readings; heated gatherings, as the old anarchist remembers, packed with the intelligentsia of

'60s and '70s Venice. Twentieth-century Venice, after all, was the birthplace (and workplace) of countless radical thinkers: avant-garde composer Luigi Nono (1924–1990); painter and pioneer of the Arte Informale movement, Emilio Vedova (1919–2006); psychiatrist and reformer Franco Basaglia (1924–1980) who first proposed the closure of psychiatric hospitals and pioneered the modern concept of mental health; philosopher and politician Massimo Cacciari (twice mayor of Venice: 1993–2000 and 2005–2010); radical politician and sometime foreign minister, Gianni De Michelis; and his older brother, the literary critic and influential publisher Cesare, just to name but a few.

Even some of Venice's most established cultural institutions were subject to this radicalism. On 18 June 1698,[3] for instance, the opening day of Venice's world-famous Biennale saw art critics arriving at the Giardini della Biennale to find baton-wielding policemen at the gates. Political activists, protesting the Vietnam War – as well as supporting students in their demands for a new education system following the Paris protests earlier that year – had taken occupation of many of the national pavilions and, in others, had turned the artworks around to face the walls, or draped anti-war banners over them.

The protests ended later that day with a police crackdown on a demo in Venice's most iconic square, Piazza San Marco. The photos of that particular June day offer a totally different image to the tourist hotspot – with its world-renowned Basilica, bell tower, and Ducal Palace – than the usual, ubiquitous holiday snaps. But as Silvano recalls, back then San Marco was no stranger to election campaign speeches or political protests, just as it hosted Carnival events and concerts; for then, the city attempted to conjugate both the residents' needs and the tourists'. Venice was a shared city.

In terms of its literary culture, there is no shortage of writing about the city. Most famously it has been written about by 'foreigners', who fell in love with her and, in some cases, decided to move here, captivated by her magic. Perhaps because of this, the literary image of the city hasn't always been as radical as that conveyed through other art forms, or through its contemporary politics, focusing as it does on its past (the city's focal point for the visitor), more than its present (the primary concern of the resident). The first half of the nineteenth and the second half of the twentieth centuries produced some of the most important 'foreigner' texts: *The Stones of Venice*, a three-volume treatise on Venetian art and architecture (as well as a glimpse at the city's society, culture and thoughts) by English art historian John Ruskin (1851-53); the American author Henry James' *Aspern Papers* (1888); the French author Marcel Proust's *A la recherche du temps perdu* (Remembrance of Things Past, 1913-27); and the American Ernest Hemingway's novel *Across the Rivers and into the Trees* (1950). Perhaps the two most iconic visions of the city came in shorter works, however: the novella *Death in Venice* (1912), by German author Thomas Mann, with its immortalisation of the Lido and the Hotel des Bains as backdrops to Gustav von Aschenbach's tragic love for the young Tadzio; and the long short story 'Don't Look Now' (1971) by British author Daphne du Maurier, about a grief-stricken married couple taking time out in the city. Both of these texts have been aided by equally iconic film adaptations (by Luchino Visconti and Nicolas Roeg respectively), and both present Venice as a city not just stuck in the past, but hauntingly, infectiously, inescapably so. Venice is an exotic trap, they seem to say, which once entered cannot be escaped.

The closest we've come to a native perspective of the city acquiring such iconic literary status is the (Cuban-born) Italian writer Italo Calvino's *Invisible Cities* (1972). For Calvino's protagonist, the explorer Marco Polo, Venice is the blueprint that overrides all other cities; nothing else can compare to its ingenuity or its oddity. In describing to Kublai Khan 55 other cities that he has allegedly seen on his journeys, Polo is really only talking about the original, his home: 'Every time I describe a city I am saying something about Venice.'

The task of writing about the Venice of today, and as a Venetian, is much trickier. Both the picture-postcard image of the city, and the crepuscular literary cliché of it, tinged with gothic morbidity, are too obvious for many writers and publishers to not carry on exploiting and perpetuating. Which is ridiculous, of course. Venice is not dead, yet. That is to say, it's not yet completely turned into a museum. There is still a beating heart to her, just as there are people still living and working here, genuinely concerned for her future.

The stories in this book address what we could call the 'other Venice'. Not the off-the-beaten-track, few-get-to-see, hidden-gems Venice, but the real, daily life of the city, as seen through the eyes of permanent residents, and having to deal with her 'extraordinary' and 'unique' problems. In many of the stories, antagonism can be detected between the two versions of the city – the 'other Venice' and the tourists' Venice – one which occasionally escalates into outright hostility: tourists are abused, robbed, insulted (even though most Venetians live entirely off them). They are stigmatised for their behaviour (everything from breaking speed restrictions on the water to walking too slowly on the streets), although, as Marilia Mazzeo gently points out in her story, 'The Casket', such behaviour was just as common in the 'ancient' Venice of 30 or 40 years ago.

Ginevra Lamberti deals with the issue of tourism in a different way. As someone who came to Venice as a student and began renting a room here, her narrator becomes trapped in a spiral of subletting to survive. Lamberti explores the city's problems in the wider, global context of property inflation, rentalisation, and the creeping invasion of the gig economy into our most personal spaces.

Roberto Ferrucci's 'Lagoon' reminds us of another problem facing the city, that of cruise ships sailing along the Grand Canal and Giudecca Canal. Here, the issue is not the tourists, but the companies bringing them here, disrupting the delicate balance of the water.

Nicola Aldani, the inspector in Michele Catozzi's story, introduces the reader to another unresolved rivalry, that between 'the city without cars' and the city with them (Mestre), the latter being home to more and more working-class people whose families have been driven out of the old city. Despite the inspector's reluctance to entirely relocate there, Mestre is in fact slowly shaking off her 'ugly sister' epithet, as its citizens try to invent a life that isn't haunted by nostalgia for the City of Water. Gianfranco Bettin, who knows both Mestre and Venice well from his political career, also deals with this urban binary, twin-homes connected by the eight kilometre-long Liberty Bridge.

Annalisa Bruni brings together a group of friends, during the kind of lockdown 'Zoom dinner' we're now all too familiar with. This particular dinner is on the 25th April, an important date for Italy (the anniversary of the liberation from fascism) and for Venice (Saint Mark's Day). The lockdown and the transformation of the city during the pandemic are also present in Cristiano Dorigo's literary voyage into Bolaño territory. Elisabetta Baldisserotto takes the reader by the hand through one of the boroughs once considered an underworld neighbourhood, Santa Marta, now 'revitalised', as architects like to say, by the conversion of certain old buildings into university faculties.

In Enrico Palandri's 'Atmospheric Conditions', a character's long solitary walks through a city he has moved to in the hope of turning a new page in his life, reflect the changes witnessed by Venice herself, and her attempts to close one chapter in her own history.

Samantha Lenarda sets her story in the year 2084, where the city has become not just a museum, but a theme park, a set for daily re-enactments, and all Venetians are reduced to the role of extras. The destiny of the city is discussed by the two young visitors, customers of Easy Venice, a 'we-think-of-everything' tourist agency for the new Lagoon-Disneyland.

For many, Lenarda's dystopia is already a reality. A string of consistently progressive, local administrations struggled to maintain the 'laboratory' that was Venice – at least until the '80s – but then the game seemed to have been given up. Now the prospect of the whole city becoming a single theme park, where you buy a ticket to enter, and nothing inside lives independently of the theme park, seems a foregone conclusion.

Some say this 'Disneyland fate' was always inevitable, but others argue it was a choice: Venice could have continued as it was, but economic interests prevailed, often encouraged by the city's residents themselves who preferred exclusively tourist-facing professions, and who are now, no doubt, cursing their decision, but unable to bite the hand that feeds them. Betting on this Disneyland fate meant sacrificing most 'normal city' activities, of course. Big cultural events (the Art Biennale and Venice Film Festival, to name just two) became less about the city and her residents, and more about putting out a red carpet for the rest of the world. The exodus of ordinary residents to Mestre, was part of this fate, as countless Venetians saw their family homes sold off – in most cases to rich Americans, and a few Brits – who barely spend one week a year in the Floating City themselves.

But blaming tourists is a cop-out; easy and inaccurate. Responsibility for Venice's sad fate lies with both the local administrators and the residents themselves. Tourism itself was never the problem; wild, unruly, uncontrolled tourism was. As Venice ossifies inevitably into the museum it always threatened to become, her few remaining residents (especially the older people and the very few families still clinging on) are in danger of becoming fossils too. The coronavirus pandemic has brutally exposed this. Hypercritically, most Venice residents have spent more time wishing the tourists would just disappear than they have demanding their local government reverse its policy of 'plunder before protection'. And when the tourists did finally disappear, due to Covid-19, the emperor's nakedness was finally recognised. The city's residents have been living almost exclusively on tourism for decades now, avoiding any investment in anything else. No one could imagine the 'fame' of the city would ever fade, just as nobody saw the virus coming.

And now Venice is alone, empty and desperately in need of a rethink. These special times, abrupt and tragic though they are, may yet bring some good; a chance to re-evaluate how Venice should function, a last chance to see what's possible. Fish are swimming in the canals again; dolphins have been spotted in the lagoon; birds not seen for decades have returned. And the water is clear! The city has started to reclaim control over herself, to heal her wounds and recover the delicate balance that had been so grossly violated.

Orsola Casagrande,
April 2021

Notes

1. John Malcolm Brinnin, *Sextet: T.S.Eliot and Truman Capote and Others* (Delacorte Press/Saymour Lawrence, New York, 1981).

2. Not to be confused with the later 'Kingdom of Italy' following the unification of Italy, Bonaparte's 'Kingdom of Italy' was a kingdom in Northern Italy (formerly the Italian Republic) in personal union with France under Napoleon I.

3. Rawsthorn Alice, 'Political Unrest of '78 still Reverberates' in *New York Times,* https://www.nytimes.com/2013/05/27/arts/27iht-design27.html

Venice, 2084

Samantha Lenarda

CAMPO SAN GIACOMETO WAS teeming with people: merchants exchanging valuable goods, captains choosing sailors for their ships, businessmen bargaining on prices. Under the arcades, stalls had been set up where the morning's haggling and transactions were recorded, and around each one merchants from all over the world waited for their turn to settle their payments.

From the piera del bando,[1] also known as The Hunchback of the Rialto, the Comandador[2] loudly proclaimed the most important decisions of the Senate and the departure of galleys for the Middle East. The everyday disorder of a noisy, busy crowd was filling the air, when, all of a sudden, a poor unfortunate man sentenced with flogging, came down from Rialto Bridge having come from San Marco, where he had atoned, and heading for San Giacometo pursued by the invectives of those crowding around him. He walked with difficulty, dragging one foot behind the other, tripping on the steps. The gendarmes tried their best to keep the crowds at a distance, as they followed him to the piera del bando where, once he had touched it, he could finally consider his punishment over.

The people at the foot of the bridge, armed with tomatoes and half-rotten lettuces, were yelling at the poor fellow, according to script. The condemned man, dressed in ragged clothes and wearing bruise makeup worthy of *The Walking Dead*, continued his slow walk, eyes downcast and looking sad, whispering to himself, 'What was I thinking, volunteering for this role!'

Henry and Alex had just arrived in Rialto and ran to find a good spot in the middle of the hustle and bustle with the other tourists, looking for some rotten vegetables to throw at the poor man who, in the meantime, had almost arrived in Campo San Giacometto. *'What a perfect moment… Hurry up, Alex.'*

'Please, Henry, no English; speak in Italian: we are Venetians now!'

Henry replied in Italian: 'Hurry up then, let's run after the criminal.'

From Rialto Bridge, sidestepping other tourists still taking pictures, they followed a wide street until it reached the little square which left them speechless: the scene was reminiscent of an eighteenth-century painting by some Venetian landscape painter. It reminded Henry of a Canaletto, but much more colourful and crowded: there were smiling young women chatting around the fountain as they filled large, earthenware jugs with water, craftsmen fixing baskets and broken chairs, noblemen talking in low voices, ladies hurrying past under the arcades, merchants bargaining under the Banco Giro, apprentices with panniers on their heads, sellers of colourful birds, water sellers, knife grinders looking for clients with their dull hum. Everywhere was wealth and ferment.

The stillness of the painting, stamped into Henry's memory, had melted into a movement of colours, the red of the cloaks, the black of the shawls, the whites of the doublets, the details of the merchants' and noblemen's costumes, everything was captured to perfection. He was ecstatic and placing the light frame of his glasses on his nose, he broke out with a 'What a fucking wonderful place! Have you seen this, Alex? It all looks so real...'

With suspicion, Alex approached the Hunchback and, knock-knock, with her fist just knocked on the plinth. 'But this is stone, real stone!... I thought it was resin.'

Henry laughed: 'What are you saying? We're not in Vegas, it's all real here, as you say. Venice has always been the same, for millennia, with its fountains, its statues, its wonderful buildings, the only thing that isn't real, but merely realistic, is the scene in front of our eyes. We are not in the eighteenth century, we are in 2084, aren't we?'

Alex was embarrassed by her ignorance and Henry, touched by her naivety, with a sweetly comforting look said: 'Let's go get an ice cream.'

They had been married for some years now, and every summer they indulged themselves with an exclusive moment, a bit of time just for them, in which to re-discover themselves. A trip was a great way to share experiences and memories, so Alex said, and this year they had chosen Venice, the city where Henry had taken his Master's in art history, and where he had lived the best year of his life, or so he had always said. 'The city where you can live and breathe art.'

They passed the Pescheria,[3] and continued towards Campo Santa Maria Mater Domini. They walked slowly, it was a beautiful spring afternoon and the sun warmed them without being too bothersome. They left behind all the confusion of the Rialto and entered the peace of the silent narrow streets. Henry watched Alex as she walked in front of him, her hair thick and black, her tall, slender figure that her baggy jeans barely did justice to. 'I feel comfortable in them,' she insisted every time she packed them into the suitcase. Henry smiled: Alex's little quirks were merits, after all, and, speeding up his pace a little, he approached her, tenderly placing his hand on her shoulder.

Licking their ice creams, they emerged into San Stae and continued towards Campo San Giacomo dall'Orio and then on to Campo dell'Accademia.

Not all of Venice was used as a set, some areas, the free ones, served as places for refreshment with ice cream parlours, bars, restaurants, some small artisan shops, tuck shops that mostly sold drinks, sliced meat in bags, and fresh bread. The shops were mostly run by mainland Venetians, who had obtained permits for retail sale inside the city, but preferred to live outside the lagoon, outside a city that they now considered only a memory. A few still lingered at the end of each shift, sitting in the secluded little bars, chatting and drinking spritz, while others hurried home late for lunch.

Henry and Alex liked to keep away from the main streets, sneaking down alleys and narrow streets: even in the smaller squares, other great scenes from Venice's past were being recreated; historical re-enactments with dozens and dozens of extras wearing costumes, all real Venetians.

After all, this is the attraction – thought Henry – *to see, all in one place, real Venetians living as they themselves had lived in this magnificent city, before the final exodus.* And turning to Alex, he said: 'Can you imagine? The people you see here today are the only Venetians you'll ever see. Maybe you'll meet one by chance, elsewhere in the world, but they would have lost their Venetian character, because they would have adapted to cars, or other lands, cities or the countryside...'

Alex looked at him sadly *'Oh Henry, I think they have a great melancholy to them...'*

And then she added: 'You know something? We did well to book overnight accommodation in the city. We would have never seen the Venetians, the real ones, if we had stayed at Easy Venice. Maybe we would have had more fun, since here there is nothing but historical reenactment after historical reenactment, but we would have missed out on something quite rare.'

Henry smiled. It pleased him to have succeeded in stimulating Alex's sensitivities.

It had been a wonderful week in which Henry had acted as her guide, telling the history of Venice, describing museums, palaces, art projects, photography shows, and Murano glass exhibitions. He told her about all the transformations the city had undergone. Alex had listened, become distracted, bored at times, but now, after that sentence, Henry understood that the trip had won her interest. It had been a great shock for her to discover that the only people who could still live in the place of their birth, was that handful of men and women. Deep down, Alex felt she had things in common with Venetians, forced to take shelter elsewhere, proud of her origins but with a void to fill. Adapting to a different place had been complex, scary, and unavoidable. She still clung to a few memories, even if they were now a couple of generations away.

They approached their hotel, the Marco Polo, once the site of an illustrious high school. The hotel had undergone a wonderfully authentic restoration and was not limited to the former high school site, but included the site of the old art school that stood opposite to it, separated by a narrow canal. The restoration had done a perfect job with both buildings, the marble of the facades had been rescued from the effects of time and returned to its original whiteness. The Venetian terrazzo floors had been restored according to the oldest artisanal techniques and the overall structure had not been inflicted with any conceptual transformations. The only variations to the original appearance were the elegant suspension bridge over the canal separating the two buildings, and a passageway similar in architecture to the Bridge of Sighs in San Marco. A miniature version of it, 'a poetic licence, a stylish homage,' people had said at its opening.

Henry and Alex loved that suspended passage and, although absolutely kitsch, they considered it an essential piece of Venetian architecture. As they looked at it from Meravegie Bridge,[4] their eyes reached further to the end of the canal, where it met the Viale della Giudecca, filled in years before to allow free access to day visitors, which was now beginning to empty of tourists eager to return to their hotels in Easy Venice on the Gronda – that thin strip of land stretching from Marghera to Fusina, built to welcome festive tourists.

They all returned en masse around 6pm, after their guided tour. The city, at night, was closed to the general public. It closed its doors at 7.30pm and all visitors with only a day ticket were sent back on their buses to Easy Venice, to splendid hotels and luxurious restaurants, or to see out the evening in the trendy nightclubs or casinos scattered throughout the holiday complexes of the Gronda.

Venice would then fall silent: not a sound could be heard; the little train and the Ferris wheel no longer running; the Production's many film sets closed; and the lagoon city remaining accessible only to the handful of residents and those tourists who had booked to stay inside, overnight – those who could afford to experience this unique place exclusively.

Alex suggested to Henry that they go and visit the wax museum as night fell. 'You'll get a bit of a shiver down your back,' he said, smiling with a hint of sarcasm. Henry, who did not like to leave things to chance, calculated the time it would have taken them to get there and back in time for dinner. Then he accepted.

They crossed the campo dell'Accademia where the impressive School of the Academy of Fine Arts stood, once a breeding ground for great ideas, for the development of cultural and artistic projects, now a trendy venue that hosted themed evenings – from Halloween, to Carnival, from spring festivals, to historical costume parties. Very popular, but with limited numbers so as to not disturb in any way the fragility and serenity of the monuments and historic buildings.

Alex suggested: 'As tomorrow is our last day, can we drop by here? Who knows what theme they've got planned. Come on...'

Henry remained vague, 'Well, there are still lots of things to see and also we haven't booked, places will be taken up until next year, I imagine.'

They passed by the bridge that crossed the Grand Canal, the only one built entirely of wood, and continued along the wide street leading into a small neighbourhood around Zattere.

The Wax Museum was located in a fifteenth-century palace overlooking the Grand Canal, decorated with pale-coloured marble and some circular medallions that embellished the façade, and accessible only through winding backstreets which, at this time of day, were illuminated by street lamps.

It was known as Ca' Dario and had a long-standing reputation for being burdened with a dark curse. According to Venetian legend, anyone who owned it either died in mysterious circumstances or ended up bankrupt. Nobody had wanted to buy it, partly out of superstition, partly due to the excessive cost of the restoration, so the Production took on the costs and turned it into a disturbing attraction.

The black wrought-iron door, intricately patterned like lace, was closed. Henry said: 'OK Google, we are Henry and Alex Kietel.' The bells to his right illuminated with a dim blue light and, after a few seconds, the door opened with a metallic and persuasive 'Welcome'.

Inside, they had read that the path would lead them upwards, following the original architecture of the building, to take in a tour of the exhibition rooms, and climb floor by floor until it reached the loggia which overlooked a splendid garden shaded by leafy horse-chestnut trees, where the museum restaurant, available only by booking online, could be found.

The altana,[5] built exclusively in wood, according to the most traditional methods, was off-limits. No visitors were allowed up there because excessive or continuous use, given the physiological deterioration of its material, had made it dangerous over time. Therefore, those who wanted to know what an altana was would need to make do with looking at it from the foot of the access ladder.

They entered and the door closed heavily behind them.

The atrium, lit by torches that created an eerie atmosphere, redolent of an Edgar Allan Poe story, housed a marble wellhead and a circular fountain that gushed silently. Scattered about stood various life-size wax statues of craftsmen intent on their work: glass masters, impiraresse,[6] impissafarai,[7] codega,[8] but also weavers, lace-makers, and carpenters skilled in boat and oar making. Inside the well, a crystal prism bathed in lasers reproduced a 3D hologram of ancient Venice, modelled on the ancient map by Jacopo de Barbari.

An inlaid marble staircase led to the floors where the nobles once lived, with some rooms displaying statues of famous Venetian painters, and others reproductions of the Serenissima's doge, the most illustrious councillors, the great leaders. The statues were many and the descriptions of their lives and deeds, declaimed by the app that Alex had downloaded on her mini-tablet, were long and detailed. They were all characters from later periods, from eras that Henry had already read about in books and that Alex didn't really want to learn about, not even from the app. 'The truth is wax museums are things of the past, there's no interaction, uff...' she complained.

'True,' Henry answered amused, 'but when was the last time you saw a museum like this? Come on, it's fascinating.'

The second floor was more compelling. Wax figures represented the politics, art and culture of Venetian society in the twentieth century. There were painters, poets, musicians, writers and politicians, the successive mayors, some of the most important ministers, magnates and entrepreneurs. The greenish LED-covered columns displayed old post-war photographs and the female voice of the app talked about a Venice that had undergone enormous industrial, cultural and social transformations over the years. On one of the pink marble walls there was a merciless monitor showing, in a tombstone graphic, the number of citizens who actually living in Venice in that century. With each decade the numbers dropped and dropped.

After inspecting each plaque and reading each interactive box, Henry said to Alex: 'Do you notice anything? On the first floor, we saw the ancient, mighty Venice, a force to be reckoned with by sea and by land, distinguished by its great naval and commercial strength. While here, in the twentieth century, as you can see, the main feature is the struggle to keep this city alive. Everyone, artists and politicians, try to revive it through different forms of protest or the preservation of traditional culture and language. Look, there are politicians trying to revive Venice according to the restoration criteria of trying to increase the number of residents. And here are some citizens, supported by various parties, fighting for a controlled rent system, and others, like this former mayor, attempting to save the city's fragile structure by raising the banks of the canals to counter high water. Provocation seemed to be what moved people during this time. Here you have artists painting surreal versions of Venice whose future is doomed to extinction. Musicians writing songs in dialect and denouncing the exodus that had already begun. Look at this text, for example: *Trezentomila lire el me ga dito, trezentomila de cossa? Ma de afito! Mi go ciapà la man de me moroso lo go ciapà e so andada via da qua...*[9] It denounces the rent increases started to get more and more serious: three hundred thousand lire in the seventies was a substantial figure for an average family. What I'm trying to say is that the theme of that century is one of citizens, fewer and fewer in number, fighting as best as they could to resist the city's gradual loss of identity, and trying to regain a lost dignity. The dignity that was lost on the first floor, to put it frankly…'

Alex laughed at the joke. 'True,' she replied, 'but if you look here, towards the end of the century, protests were already fading. Fewer prominent musicians, even fewer artists… and as for politics… bah. The innovators, those who believed that real change could be made or things could be shaken, they came before, and had all grown up and matured in the time between the sixties and the eighties, right?'

Henry reflected on Alex's words and responded: 'To me, the thing that stands out is what the graph on this table shows: since the 1990s, Venetian residents, crushed by the economic transformation that increasingly linked jobs to exorbitant all-consuming mass tourism, dwindled in number and tended to leave the city, to make new homes in the more affordable Mestre or its surroundings. Their work, gradually but irreversibly moved to the mainland too. It seems to me that, as early as the end of the twentieth century, the exodus was a done deal and there were few left to protest it…'

Given its delicate structure, the museum had been set up to host only a small number of visitors per day. Henry and Alex felt as they were alone and, chatting amiably in loud voices, they ascended further.

The third floor was made up of four separate rooms, which most likely had been old bedrooms. The whole floor was dedicated to the 21st century and opened with some wax figures representing the city's most recent mayors. The second room was reserved for the MOSE project,[10] the largest engineering project carried out during those years, with detailed descriptions of how the dam worked to stave off the high tide. The 3D rendering moved slowly in its virtual tour of the dams and near the large monitor stood a wax statue of the mayor who had pioneered the project. And just to the left of that, beside a mullioned window, another statue of the same mayor, this time with his head down, in handcuffs and, on the wall behind him, hundreds of newspaper articles from the time, scanned and arranged in a huge collage, describing the scandal of bribes that surrounded the dam's construction. A disconcerting scene that made Alex chuckle: 'So that's why it took them so long to get it working!'

The tour continued in the next room with a statue of the latest mayor, smiling in her blue suit, showing the new MOSE project finally working with all the necessary modifications and technical specifications.

In the final room stood the same mayor, this time shaking hands with the owner of the Easy Venice company and behind them another screen with a 3D rendering of the layout Venice had assumed for the last twenty years. Next to them, sporting a pair of octagonal spectacles and a fur hat, stood John Kuy, the American musician who had taken up residence in the city for some years now and had dedicated one of his most famous trap songs to Venice.

'Very little has happened in 21st century, has it?' Alex said.

'Eh?!' Henry replied, a little dazed. 'Loads has happened, what are you talking about? They've implemented a million urban improvements, completed great engineering projects. I guess you mean there's been no writers, painters, or artists... apart from, maybe, this trapper.'

'I don't know,' Alex began, 'maybe Venetians no longer care about fighting for their city, protesting or showing their discontent. Maybe, in the end, all these tourists suited them, after all, Venetians have been taking advantage of them for at least thirty years.'

Henry wasn't surprised by Alex's cynicism, but he was annoyed by her offhand summary and the lack of detailed reasoning and he tried to dig deeper: 'What makes you say that?'

Alex took a detour back along the walls of the two previous rooms, where the photographs of a Venice under assault, marred by uncontrolled tourism were exhibited. The images showed the time when the mass of people entering the city could no longer be managed: huge crowds perched all over the monuments eating McDonald's burgers, sitting on wells that doubled as tables for half-empty plastic cups, sprawling on the steps of bridges or lying down to rest in the middle of the Procuratie of San Marco, lost, bewildered and tired. The colours were saturated, violent and enough to instil in the visitor a sense of total disorder in stark contrast to the order of the scale models and 3D renderings, clean and sterilised, displayed in the later rooms, showing a Venice controlled and managed with competence.

'Henry, Venice is a fragile and delicate city, right? And it's unbelievable it was ever threatened the way it was in these photos? Right, so... I ask myself: who treated this city like shit? The mayors, yes. The councillors, sure. The political parties, of course. But Henry, why were its citizens also complicit in just selling it to the highest bidder? Why didn't they rent the houses to other residents? Why did they accept all this? Huh? It's always convenient to blame others, come on... you taught me that!' and she gave a sly chuckle.

Henry frowned. 'Don't you think it was really hard to respond? For example, look at this photo of the former Faculty of Arts building, below, the caption reads: *today a permanent exhibition of the works of Arthur Fritzdielmann*, or look at this building, once home to the Education Department, now one of Venice's most desirable hotels. Which means that the municipality itself, right here at the start of the 21st century, began selling itself off to private corporations in order to raise cash, right? So if political trends only shift in one direction, it's understandable that citizens follow the same path. If the city itself no longer has the strength to offer an alternative and bows to the highest bidder instead of creating policies to defend its citizens, then it is understandable that all those who lived here adapted to that offer.'

'Sure, and is it OK for them to open B&Bs in every apartment, to rent rooms upon rooms without control, until the city is transformed into a giant dormitory?' Alex replied, pointing to a series of images that spoke for themselves: doors with bells next to which electronic locks had appeared to allow entry to the converted B&Bs and holiday apartments, automated offices scattered around the city offering do-it-yourself check-in and check-out, alongside images of apartments with closed shutters, worn by time.

Henry, speechless, thought back to the second floor, the one exhibiting the twentieth century. It still seemed to him a proud century, full of initiatives. At that point, a monitor, hanging almost transparent, near the statue of John Kuy caught his attention. 'Look here, not all of the 21st century was as dry as you think.' On the screen appeared the names of all the charities that had worked for the city, all those that had taken care of cleaning its soiled monuments, of dredging its waste-clogged canals, all those that had kept its traditions alive by giving their labour free of charge for the conservation of the city's popular festivals, those who had proposed ideas, projects to try to improve Venice's destiny.

'Yes, yes, they had no one else to call on,' Alex replied firmly, and with a clarity that surprised Henry said: 'It is obvious that in the 21st century there have been no movements, other than attempts to stem a problem that was already overflowing. You must see the difference between this century and the last one! Back then, the struggles and protests for the future of the city transcended demographics, cut across politics and culture. In this century, the struggle is just superficial, no one really pays attention to the complaints, and politics is entirely detached from the needs of the people!'

'I don't know, Alex.' Henry sounded discouraged. 'It does seem strange, not to see a single prominent painter, writer, or politician, someone who, as in previous years, left a mark…'

'That's because you being your usual windbag self, even when you are on holiday you're a professor!' Alex laughed at him and added, gesticulating wildly: 'In any case, it's not true, here is your important politician, the last mayor, what's her name… ah yes… Mariele Dorio, she's the one who started and promoted the whole Easy Venice project and it's to her that we owe our very being here, you know?'

She kneeled down laughing, her hands clasped together, in front of the wax statue and said in a feigned pleading voice: 'Thanks Mariele, thank youuuuuuuu.'

A moment later she was already on the loggia taking a selfie with her tablet. The sky was still bearing the colours of the sunset, slowly diluting into the dark blue of the evening, and the glow of the candles and street lamps was warming up gradually. The tables in the garden restaurant were already set and there was the faint scent of aromatic herbs.

The evening was cool and Alex headed back in. 'Shall we go down?' she proposed. 'I'm hungry.'

As they descended the marble staircase, Henry thought that ultimately Alex was not wrong; if the city had been transformed this way, it had happened because it was probably the only real way to preserve its values, to keep its treasures intact, to spare it the risk of suffering further damage.

'Of course, we must not forget,' Henry considered, 'that this whole museum is an obvious marketing stunt designed to enhance the work done in recent years by Hans Lieder Produktion, to glorify its Venice rescue work. It's a blatantly self-referential representation of the struggle between good and evil inviting us to believe that Lieder's operation was the only viable solution. And who knows, maybe that's the way it went... but I can't help thinking how sad it is to see the most powerful force in the Mediterranean slowly transformed into a ghost town.'

He took one step after another, caressing the pale marble wall with his hand and lingering a few seconds with each step to give space for his reflections. *Today I glimpsed the slow process of the end of a great civilisation and its legitimacy... And the Venetians? Well, with their adaptability they will have learned to live somewhere else. The point is not the Venetians* – he mused – *but the death of a city that now stands empty, uninhabited, without anyone to gives it the depth of a lived place or the respect it deserves.*

Alex was already waiting for him at the bottom of the stairs. 'God, you're such a snail...'

'No, I was thinking,' Henry muttered

'What now, come on?' Alex said impatiently.

Henry smiled. 'I was thinking that you're right. Enough of the museums and the old stuff. After dinner, how about we swing by the San Marcuola Casino, at Palazzo Vendramin Calergi, one of the oldest casinos in the world.'

'Yaaay!' Alex chirped.

Notes

1. Literally 'the stone of notice', a stone plinth present in some Medieval Italian cities, from which new laws were proclaimed. In Venice, there were two, one in Piazza San Marco and one near the Rialto.

2. The Comandador was the person who read (or shouted) out the sentences of the court to the public. He would stand either on Rialto Bridge or on a high place, such as the piera del bando, to attract people's attention.

3. The fish market.

4. Also known as the Bridge of Wonders, located in the borough of Dorsoduro, near the Accademia. It takes its name from the family Maraviglia, who lived in the vacinity for many generations.

5. A platform located on the highest part of a Venetian building. Unlike terraces and balconies, altanas do not protrude from the main building.

6. Women whose job it was to string together glass beads into necklaces, etc.

7. A man whose job it was to manually light the city's street lamps.

8. A lantern-bearing guide or protective escort for wealthier visitors, merchants or noblemen in medieval and Renaissance Venice, taking them to and from theatres, cafés or the docks at night, warding off thieves until they were safe inside.

9. *Three hundred thousand? Three hundred thousand for what? Rent! And I took my boyfriend by the hand and left...* from the song 'Trezentomila' (1981) by Michela Brugnera.

10. Experimental Electromechanical Module ('MOdulo Sperimentale Elettromeccanico'), a project intended to protect Venice from flooding, through integrated rows of mobile gates designed to isolate the Venetian Lagoon temporarily from the Adriatic Sea during high tides. With work starting in 2003, its construction was subject to multiple delays, cost overruns and scandals, and missed its expected completion date of 2018, but is expected to be fully functional by October 2021.

Venice is my Mother

Cristiano Dorigo

*The package had been sent from Venice, where Archimboldi,
or so he said in a short letter enclosed with the manuscript,
had been working as a gardener...*

*Archimboldi's address was on Calle Turlona in
Cannaregio, and the baroness guessed correctly that the street
couldn't be too far from the train station...*

Roberto Bolaño, 2666

WHEN I WRITE I don't know where the words come from, nor
which direction they will take. There are those who write
already knowing everything, and those who set off from an
initial intuition and let their fingers be their guide: I belong to
the second category.

To write about Venice puts me in an ambivalent position:
on one side, there's the advantage of already knowing the
subject so well; on the other, there's the risk of saying
something that has already been said, or worse, the risk of
trying too hard in the pursuit of originality.

So when they proposed the project to me I accepted
immediately, even if I didn't know what I was going to write;
it was only afterwards that I had the epiphany: Venice is my
mother.

The elements: a city, a maternal feeling, water, senses, a house number.

A note about the house number: I've read a lot of reviews of *2666*, the last novel by Roberto Bolaño, an author I love. With regard to the meaning of that titular number, there are many hypotheses, several questions, and no certainties. The fact that the main character, around whom the five parts of the novel revolve, had been in Venice made me curious: this is one of the few cities, as far as I know, that has house numbers that go this high, and I wondered if there could be a connection. I thus began looking for this number in each sestiere – Venice is historically divided into six neighbourhoods called 'sestieri' – and I discovered that this figure is reached in only five of them: five like the chapters of his novel; five like the senses. Bolaño's books are made up of an infinite number of stories. Venice too has an infinite number of stories, of mothers, of waters, and is a sensorial experience. Stories echoed by memory and the deaf voice of the dead; stories that only the living can tell: five house numbers, five sestieri, five senses, five stories.

Venice still follows the traditional house numbering system invented before the nineteenth century; in each sestiere, the numbering grows progressively around each block, then it resumes from the adjacent one, until the whole sestiere is covered.

Cannaregio 2666, bora,[1] hearing – Venice 2020

Today a very strong bora is blowing. The water ripples and almost seems to shiver with the small, sharp waves passing over its surface; the line of washing stretches and flaps in time to the rhythm of the gusts; the shutters slam against the windows; the wind rises and drops, in shrill or guttural whistles, imposing itself indifferent to how it may sound. The sky rapidly changes colour, mood and light, in a perpetual play of shadow and shade.

At this moment, we must coexist with a powerful, paradoxical and invisible force: a microscopic virus has brought the whole world to its knees, revealing its excesses, frailties, and madness. But it's been necessary for us to experience it to know that this is so: that boiling our lives down to an infinite series of bad habits would have brought us – by us, I mean humanity – to the brink of existential collapse. This is true in general as well as in the specific: the city was on the verge of asphyxiating from gluttony, overflowing with people; an anthill, a sad postcard, a simulacrum of society as whole.

These days are a messy, empty time and, in my head, the image that comes closest to summing it up is that of a glass globe with a tiny house inside that, once you turn it upside down, releases hundreds of little snowflakes: the impression is that everyone is inside there, in that transparent shell that lets you see what's inside, but not touch it.

During these days of quarantine, I have left for work almost every day. Here in Venice, silence has returned, holy, rare, and enchanted. Even the colour has reset back to its primaeval palette, to the transparent green of the canals, to the rich blue of the sky, to the transparency of the air. Despite this, even while aware of the privilege of enjoying such beauty exclusively, the switch from being full to empty was a hard blow to take. In the days before the total lockdown, the streets and squares, free of tourists, seemed also emptied of energy, revealing the original crime in all its naked crudeness: if things had carried on as they were, they risked transforming a lively urban environment into a soulless shopping mall.

An interlude was needed, a pause in the perpetual noise of the trolley-cases, from the omnipresent hum in every kind of idiom; we needed complete silence, the kind you only hear in the middle of the night, the kind that allows you to hear the sound of your own footsteps echoing between the sides of the street, that even during daylight makes you look afresh at things, returning you to a type of love whose sense and meaning are perhaps intangible and yet carnal, powerful, embedded deep.

The bora is a wind that dishevels, that changes the status quo, that welcomes new things more than existing ones. We'll wait and see what happens, prepared to coexist with new demands, old habits, endless shared uncertainties. This is what I was thinking while walking in solitude towards the street that hosted the number 2666. From Santa Lucia Station, heading through Lista di Spagna and Campo San Geremia brings you to Guglie Bridge, and the Ghetto, beyond which lies Fondamenta dei Ormesini – not far from Calle Turlona mentioned in the excerpt –, along which can be found Calle del Forno: at the end of that stands the fateful door.

San Marco 2666, eating disorder, taste – Venice 1969, 2009

As I arrived in Piazzale Roma, I parked the motorbike, chained up the helmet, and shouldered my rucksack. I started to walk thinking about something a dear friend had told me about a friend of his, whose daughter suffered from an eating disorder. Years ago I wrote a short story that addressed this issue: it was a route across the city that lead to the Santi Giovanni e Paolo Hospital – right next to a basilica of the same name which, along with the Frari basilica, represented one of the largest and most imposing medieval buildings in Venice. The hospital entrance is a spectacular Renaissance building that has been home to the Scuola Grande di San Marco for more than five centuries.

In my short story, during the walk that leads him there, the girl's father talks about the many types of food he eats along the way.

The destination of *this* chapter, however, is somewhere else, in another neighbourhood, but part of the route is the same, and it takes me back to when I was a child – switching to the original mother-son roles – and it contains some of the elements I wrote about in the brief opening passage.

There was a time when Venice was an inhabited city, animated by local people and businesses – unlike these days when the lack of both embarrasses it, distorting its essence, blurring its uniqueness into an idealised place, instead of a real town populated by people rather than extras.

And it was during that era that, as a child, I played alone along the canal while my mum was at the hairdresser.

I'm not sure of the details, but I believe I snuck out of the shop without anyone seeing me: a tiny little creature taking advantage of everyone's eyes being hidden by the Martian helmet-shaped hairdryers – the not-so-young-anymore will get this reference while others won't – and being distracted by the chatter, which, at this juncture in the late sixties, was dense with heavy words.

I don't remember how, but I fell into the water. One moment I was enjoying the cool caress of a breeze, the next I was immersed in water. What I do remember is the muffled sound, bubbles coming out of my mouth and my nose, and a soft fluctuation that lifted me up and down. I wasn't worried, being busy staring at the world underwater, giving myself up to the giant aquarium that I was now inside. I was floating inertly in a state of unconscious peace, surrounded by the numbing, dark, green, salty liquid. It only lasted a few seconds, and yet time seemed to have been diluted, extended, in that moist peace.

Interrupting that soft aquatic interlude came the sudden downward intrusion of a dull crash from above. Arriving as powerfully as if being shot from a rifle: a hand, followed by the whole arm; it headed towards me, grabbed me, secured me to itself and then lifted me, an imaginary piston, putting my feet back on the canal side.

My mother, warned by who knows who, ran out the hairdresser shop, screaming, a picture of pure emotion: joy and anguish in curlers; happiness and despair at the same time.

She hugged me so tight I was almost suffocated with love.

Without knowing it, she hated me for how much she loved me.

This is just one of many fragments of memory from those early years, when I lived close to Santa Marta, in the Mendicoli neighbourhood, where my father and my aunt still live. I remember that in the sweet, serene summer evenings of my childhood, the women would take out their chairs and start to chat to keep themselves company, exchanging news and opinions, facing the hot weather together.

At the time, Venice was much more inhabited, lived in. If an episode like the one I just recounted happened today, there wouldn't be any story to tell as the author wouldn't have been there: maybe there wouldn't have even been a hand to save the tiny, unwitting diver.

From Santa Marta, I headed for the San Marco house number. Santa Margherita, San Barnaba, Accademia, Campo Santo Stefano, San Maurizio. Right here, over a shop, is the number 2666. By pure coincidence, it was right in front of where my dear friend – the one who told me about his friend – had lived for a few years every summer. Which is why I decided to end this passage with an excerpt from the final part of the short story I mentioned at the beginning.

...The night here will be long and very short as usual.

I will hear few voices.

Maybe just my own.

Updating you on the daily menus.

And I will hear the electronic beep and hum of machinery certifying life.

As I already explained, despite everyone's opinion, I will keep asking you to rely on me.

They tell me you can't hear.

I'm not interested in them understanding.

I know that between one word and another, between each description of what I ate and drank, you will feed yourself too.

Nobody has understood our balance yet, our secret that will see us smiling with a private happiness.

They may not know that since the disease started I have carefully followed every tiny fluctuation in your weight.

To make sure that what you lost didn't disappear, I accumulated it; to make sure the energy you dispelled by vomiting didn't disappear, I gained it, eating and putting on weight by the same amount you lost. Exactly, exactly.

I have grown precisely, mathematically symmetrical to your shrinking.

And we are still perfectly balanced.

The sum of our weight is exactly as it was before.

The sum of our love is exactly as it was before...

San Polo 2666, high tide, touch – Venice, 2019

On the evening of 12 November 2019, the tide forecast was worsening by the hour. In the house on the mainland where I live, we stayed awake, fascinated until the wind stopped howling: it was a furious south-easterly wind that seemed able to bend trees, pressing violently on the windows, testing their resilience; it was a bad omen. We were worried for our friends living in ground floor apartments, in buildings flooded with saltwater; but also for others, on higher floors, where water surged out of toilet bowls; and we thought about the shopkeepers forced to lift all their stock to higher and higher ground, exhausted to the point of resignation, finally abandoning themselves to the damp fate that had befallen them. And I thought about my 85-year-old dad and my 90-year-old aunt, alone in their homes when the disaster struck. Late into the night, we responded with compulsive, symptomatic gestures: we kept looking at smartphones, tablets, computers, at the centre of our modern lives, connected live to a phenomenon as old as the world itself.

A mournful night, dampened by a process of osmosis, thickened by a few tormented hours sleeping then waking up again, distressed by sympathetic anxiety, by dignified resigned fraternity.

The following day, once I checked that my veci[2] were fine – my aunt had slept through the whole thing – I walked across the city to reach that fateful house number, as I had planned.

The tide rises and falls every six hours: it recedes and swells according to the influence of the moon, therefore it is literally lunatic. And maybe so am I, and all Venetians, being so used to loving it anyway, to taking it just as it is, with all its virtues and vices, sold as seen – and *lived*. I set off anyway, despite the inauspicious forecasts, predicting discouraging water levels, and so it happened: and I got soaked up to my thighs, since the tide had risen again blown by a violent wind.

I recorded voice notes on my mobile phone, being unable to write, wandering astounded, anxious. When I ran into someone, we exchanged conspiratorial, understanding, resigned glances.

What loomed over everything, in my opinion, was the feeling of fusion with the city, with its elements, with stones, water, dirt, air: I was stones, water, dirt, air; as well as sorrow, affection, a disconsolate gratitude, a dignified confusion, a silent peace between one wound and another.

Transcribing the voice notes:

> We look at each other differently when we are soaking wet; the maternal city contains us, bringing us back to the amniotic fluid, to the prenatal phase, when things are simply what they are, and we become happy creatures obeying the laws of nature.
>
> We proceed slowly, carefully measuring the length of each step to avoid splashing others, throwing Venetian curses at those who splash you, when every step creates a splash of some kind. There's an unwritten code of behaviour assumed by those living in this city: it has to do with how to walk around in often crowded places, narrow, packed. You need to allow yourself some air, mimic a kind of elegant dance when you're not completely crushed by strangers who don't realise that to live as a biped requires order, respect and reciprocity. This applies to any given day, and even more during high tide. It applies also when it rains and you approach someone in a narrow street: one lifts the umbrella, the other lowers and half closes it, bringing it closer, parallel to the body, along the hip and leg – it's an atavistic gesture, not exactly modern, a chivalrous act, going back to when a man did his utmost to lavish courtesies on a lady. In any case, it only works when the tallest one lifts the arm to the shorter one pass under.

I pass slowly through San Rocco – first the Scuola Grande and the church, then the majestic Basilica dei Frari, one of the most solemn of the whole city. I cross Archivio Bridge – one of the four most important State Archives of the world – then take the Sottoportego de Ca' Zen, turning off into a beautiful hidden square, a cul-de-sac: Corte Moro. Here, over a green front door, is the fateful number.

I'm soaking wet – 'bombo' in Venetian dialect – but happy. I get a brief shudder of excitement every time I manage to find the location of the house number in each respective sestiere – where even the satnavs fail, giving wrong directions – being thus even closer to Roberto Bolaño.

The evening of 12 November 2019 saw the second highest tide of all time: 187cm, just 7cm lower than in 1966. The year ended with almost 50 instances of high tides above 80cm, which led to San Marco being frequently flooded, at least partially. Climate change exponentially increases weather phenomena that would have once been considered atypical, making them typical, even normal.

But you can only live for so long with the water that invades houses, shops, lives, thoughts, perspectives.

Castello 2666, horizon, vision – Venice 2003

Venice is a complex, multifaceted city, quite extensive especially in terms of population size. It's made up of several parts – if we looked at satellite photos of the city, we would see three large entities separated by a stretch of water, joined by a thin thread, surrounded by scattered dots of different sizes, ending with two long strips in the east. As I write this first passage I find myself in one of those two, Lido.

It's a summer afternoon by the sea, I'm observing the

water: primordial mother, fluid necessity. For a while, I stare at the horizon uniting the elements, a thin, barely distinguishable line in that infinite blue. I smell the saltiness, caressing the olfaction and passing down the throat tickling the taste buds. And I listen to the perpetual motion of the water becoming foam on the shore and withdrawing, turning into liquid again.

I sit down and watch: one minute, five, ten.

I relax my shoulders, which I realise have been tense.

I sit comfortably, loosening up the taut muscles, stretched like high-tension cables.

I'm surrounded by people whose chattering seems endless. Despite this, here I rest my mind, calm my thoughts, smooth out the corners, betray all sense of haste, abhor what's pointless.

At some point I stand up and start to walk slowly, the water rising up my legs, giving me a slight shiver. I swim until I'm exhausted and once I reach the open sea far from the noise, I turn over and float on my back. I remain like this hoping to reconnect to that feeling that I sometimes catch, but more often miss, of a foetus swimming, protected by the mother's body. Here, alone at last, I feel the root of regret that has always troubled me and always will. I lived in perfection and, like everyone else, I lost it forever, corrupted by my coming into the world. I immerse my ears in the water and I let the dullness of the sounds take me away from the hum. I close my eyes and with a pure act, I join that lack, that generous belly, that silence, that perfect intimacy.

I go back to it, that which is just a memory now rather than a presence, that which is metaphysics, an imaginary space to take shelter in.

One way to make up for the absence of the mother is to go back to a place where there was no need for words or gestures, only for a presence.

I float as if I'm dead, and I am reborn.

Then I go back ashore, lie down, listen to the perpetual motion of the waves, let myself go to the heat of the sun in its liquid numbness.

I put my clothes back on calmly and I set off to the vaporetto station walking in a state of grace – I wouldn't know how to measure a period of time free from thoughts and anxieties. Once onboard, the serenity dissipates, defeated by the crowd. I get off at the Arsenale stop and I set off along the canal side. It's hot, my breathing slows down, I feel the sun start to warm my head and back as I walk in silence. I hear someone calling my name, and turn around and behind me see a friend of mine waving: he's on his sandolo,[3] rowing. I ask him for a ride, so I can paddle a little too. In a few minutes we turn into the Rio della Ca' di Dio, continuing to where the Rio dei Scudi and the Rio Santa Ternita begin. I tell him to drop me off at the foot of the Ponte dei Scudi, where I say goodbye, climb over the railing, enter the street of the same name, and I find number 2666.

Dorsoduro 2666, absences, smell – Venice 2001

Dorsoduro is the sestiere where I was born and where I lived the first years of my life, before moving with my family to Mestre. This is where most of our relatives lived and, after about fifteen years, my parents came back too. This is where, one day many years ago, I lived through an odyssey: not the first one, not the last for sure, but one of the most significant.

My parents' house is a few minutes away from Piazzale Roma. That day, as I arrived I felt a pang in my heart and a rumbling in my belly: the body expresses itself with a visceral language, I thought.

When I was little, this area had been a centre for small businesses and socialising. Local people met here, when there still were locals and the place throbbed with life. Now silence envelopes the houses, wrapping them in a nostalgic embrace.

When I rang the bell my father opened the door; I was struck by an impulse to rush upstairs and, at the same time, by a sudden need to escape.

My brother and my mother were in the living room which also served as a triage room.

As soon as I entered I approached her, greeting her with a shy kiss on the cheek.

She had her eyes closed, and when she opened them, you could see the pain as well as the morphine acting on both her body and consciousness, softening and anaesthetising it, despite her surprising vigilance.

She had greeted me with a voice that I hardly recognised, filtered by the battle inside her body: a jumble of cells and molecules fighting furiously in silence.

While I was there I would cast frequent glances at her: she, who had assembled me day by day inside her, when I was just a thought in progress, a future engraved in the flesh of a young woman.

Looking at her, I had a clear mnemonic vision of when she hosted me in her round belly, of when I floated in her silent sea. Her legs were a heartbreaking sight: wrapped with a kind of cling film that needed to be changed regularly, since the lower halves, from the knee down, kept secreting a transparent liquid similar to water.

That liquid hypnotised me: amniotic fluid backwashing.

I would have liked to find that watery peace again, instead of remaining in the solid torment that haunted me.

Suddenly the TV interrupted its broadcast to show images of a plane crashing into a skyscraper. Our astonishment acted like a jolt: we all re-emerged from the torpor hanging in the air. She asked if we could explain what was happening. We tried to tell her, but maybe she couldn't believe our words, so she opened her eyes to see the impossible for herself.

I looked at her legs that kept discharging fluid, and I imagined it was energy leaving her body. I wanted to approach her, touch her, give substance and priority to the sense of touch, but I couldn't: I should have reduced that distance before it became regret. Everyone's attention had suddenly been drawn to the TV screen: there was smoke coming out of the skyscraper. I experienced a kind of relief for what I felt, and I was ashamed: but it was the relief of being able to share the precariousness of life. The inevitable widening of private, personal pain, making it public and shared, does not soothe it, it merely distracts us with the pain of the others. Pain produces isolation, makes us selfish, mean, in need of compassion.

Then another plane arrived and crashed into the other tower. The point of collision was definitely lower this time, compared to the previous one.

Black smoke poured out from the first tower; the presenter seemed to have gone mad, he didn't know what to say and was chattering on as if babbling or stammering in some way. My brother and I looked at each other in dismay, stony-faced.

We turned simultaneously to see she had opened her eyes. She closed them again immediately, uttering words that seemed a kind of self-prophecy, in a crumpled voice with a dry throat: 'It's the end of life.'

From one of the towers you could see a small black spot descending. It was a man who had stepped into the void from a skyscraper on fire. For a brief moment, I caught the silence hanging in the air. A heavy, exhausting silence, a premonition of the speechlessness that inhabits loneliness, pain and grief.

She reopened her eyes a little, she was looking at us, and in a whisper she uttered these few words: 'I wish I could comfort you, but I can't even comfort myself. I don't have the energy.' Before closing her eyes again, realising that we were all looking at her, she nodded towards the TV.

The first tower was collapsing.

It was a catastrophe of dust, rubble, smoke, weakness, hate, defeat.

I felt my left leg buckling, making me lose my balance.

Then the other tower, the same scene in slow motion.

The other leg gave way.

The towers were collapsing and I was falling too, in a paradoxical tragic simultaneity.

I looked at the towers, then at my mother, feeling an abnormal pain gripping my flesh, twisting my organs and shaking my head.

I looked at the indescribable cloud of dust at the base: it covered everything, hid everything; it seemed to come out of the screen and enter people's houses, nostrils, lungs until we couldn't breath anymore.

I thought about the outrage, the massacre, the number of deaths.

I thought about how my mother was leaving us and how all of those deaths, all of that obscene, pornographic display of despair was nothing compared to what I was feeling, revealing to me the true nature of suffering, something inevitable, uncontrollable, omnipotent.

And it was nothing like what I imagined, thought, believed, assumed it would be; no, it was much worse and much better, it was both material and spiritual, both prayer and a blasphemy, an end and a beginning, everything and nothing.

Crawling towards the armchair, I took her hand, and caressed it with my cheek.

I felt that she was leaving us and there was nothing I could do.

I knew that it was like that, and so it had to be, and I finally felt a kind of relief, a lightness, a sweetness, a peace, a fullness, an abandonment.

Years have passed since then, but I still feel the need to write about it. Maybe because I've never forgotten what I smelled in the days following that tragic event. The sense of smell is one that preserves the unconscious memory, and every time I think about it, write about it, it returns like clockwork.

The house number is only five minutes away from my father's house. I cross the Ponte Dea Piova, then pass through Campo de l'Azolo Rafael, then another bridge, Calle Lunga San Barnaba, yet another bridge and after a few metres, on the right, opposite to a parish recreation centre are the house numbers 2665 and 2667: there is no 2666. It must have been erased by the wear and tear of time and never been rewritten. It is there, though, as a kind of invisible energy. It had been there but now it was missing, prompting me to go back to that September 11, 2001, when my mother was still there.

And now I miss her.

Fun fact: in the National Annual Record for 1935, house number 2666 in Dorsoduro is assigned to Zattere and to the Società di Navigazione Adriatica, the Adriatic sailing society. Well, my father was born in 1935 and for a few years before his retirement he worked at the Adriatica's premises.

One of the philological theories interprets this number as 'twice the number of the beast': the lack of the house number in question could be due to the intervention of a priest, I guess, for just this reason.

Notes

1. A strong, cold, dry north-east wind that blows in the upper Adriatic.
2. Venetian word, meaning 'elders'.
3. A traditional, flat-bottomed Venetian boat, smaller and less ornate than a gondola, and without the benches and high steel prow, but like the gondola rowed while standing up.

The Casket

Marilia Mazzeo

AT TEN PAST SIX on a May morning in 2018, Mr Guido Zane got out of bed and, before anything else, threw open the windows and shutters of his room. There he stood for a while contemplating a truly remarkable view. Mr Zane lived on the third floor of a house in the borough of Dorsoduro in Campiello Barbaro, a small square known for being one of the prettiest and most picturesque corners of Venice. A corner that features in many paintings and films. He had lived there for more than forty years, that is, since his third child was born and the family had moved into a more spacious apartment. Mr Zane was now eighty-two: a small, old man, thin, if not downright skinny, like so many men of his age, but with something good in his smile. To see him wearing that good smile, those blue eyes with that mild, insecure expression, no one would have guessed he was capable of great anger.

Mr Zane was a painter. All his life, he had done nothing but paint: and he had always done it in the traditional way, with canvases and brushes, oils and turpentine. At the end of the twentieth century, he had dabbled in acrylics, but with little satisfaction.

His studio did not overlook Campiello Barbaro, but an internal garden. It was a bright and quiet room, silence and light being, of course, the most important things.

Campiello Barbaro – with its endless coming and going of tourists on their way to the Basilica della Salute – was not quiet enough; it had never been, but time had made it worse.

The birds chirped. The sun was shining, although still low on the horizon and invisible behind the roofs. The sky was deep blue, not a cloud in sight. It was one of those perfect, sweet, enchanting spring mornings, that would fill even an eighty-two-year-old painter with a sense of gratitude and joy. With admiration, Mr Zane greeted the small square that he had painted so often, with the canal's line of deep green down one side, the fountain that had always been there, and the green flowerbed in the centre which, on the contrary, had been added, for some reason, about twenty years ago. He appreciated the elegant curve of the bridge, and the wall of ancient bricks, decorated with swirls of salt that surrounded the rear garden of Palazzo Dario. He stared at the roofs for a long time, the trees, the masegni[1] and the chimneys, especially the beautiful vase-shaped chimneys that opened up to the sky like corollas. The only shops in the campiello[2] were two small art galleries, currently closed. Nobody was stirring, not even dog walkers or street cleaners.

He dressed impatiently, without paying attention to what he was actually wearing. Spring had been rather rainy until that day. Now that it was bright and clear, Mr Zane couldn't wait to go out and enjoy it. He went into the kitchen and made himself a coffee, added milk and sugar, and drank it at the window, anticipating his walk. His daughter had ordered him not to go out before the arrival of Alina, the cleaning lady. Alina would arrive at nine with the shopping and her first task was always to prepare breakfast for him. But Mr Guido Zane could not wait. As the saying goes, the morning has gold in its mouth and all this freshness, serenity and birdsong would soon disappear. After nine, the first intrepid groups of tourists would start to pass by, and he tried to avoid tourists if he could. He paused for a moment looking at his overcoat: was it still necessary? The day seemed warm; but, being uncertain, he finally put it on. He could always take it off and carry it folded over his arm.

Mr Zane's morning walks were always the same. First, he headed for the Basilica della Salute, which stood in all its glory a short distance away. He loved it as one might love a wife, who, despite knowing for many years, you are still able to discover something new about each morning. He had painted it many times, over the years, from different angles and in different lights, finding it the same each time and yet different: the immense portals; the towering columns; the many statues; the grandiose dome; and under the dome those great, bizarre curls of white marble that resembled the foam of crashing waves, distinguishing it from all the other baroque churches in the world; and all so wonderfully reminiscent of a sea creature, an urchin, a jellyfish, an octopus.

His walk then continued towards Punta della Dogana, a panoramic terrace overlooking the middle of San Marco basin, from which he could admire the incomparable spectacle of the city resting on the blue-green waters of the lagoon: on one side, the Piazza, the Palace and the Campanile; on the other, the island of San Giorgio and the façade of the Redentore, like the backdrop of the most beautiful stage set in the world. The tide was high that day and the waves pounded happily at his feet, against the Istrian stone; the wind-tossed lagoon was already crowded: numerous boats overloaded with white sacks, which Mr Zane knew to be filled with sheets washed in the mainland's laundries and on their way back to the hotels, and even more numerous boats loaded with bottles, an incredible quantity of bottles – mineral water, beer, drinks of all kinds – also destined for the thousands of hotels and restaurants in the city.

Beside him, by contrast, there was still no one. He enjoyed the view in solitude and was pleased to have gone out early. It was not the same elbowing your way between crowds of noisy tourists, with their ridiculous hats, bumbags and shorts, whatever the season, with red noses from too much sun, and above all, always with phone in hand, frantically taking pictures and selfies without respite, when it would have been far more appropriate to just remain silent and still and to look, look and look again.

Satisfied, Mr Zane turned the corner and set off for the Zattere, but stopped immediately. Petrified. Someone was sleeping there. Two men, stuffed into their sleeping bags, were lying against the wall of the Dogana, the old Customs building. He approached them cautiously to take a better look: they were young, clean-looking, not homeless. The sleeping bags were definitively dirty, but the heads that emerged were covered in short blond hair, neatly trimmed. Under their heads, acting as pillows, were two backpacks. Next to those, two pairs of trainers, fairly new, some paper bags and two big, glass beer bottles, empty.

Mr Zane became angry. He began to give the two young men gentle kicks. 'You can't do that!' he shouted. 'It is forbidden! Wake up! It is forbidden to sleep on the street!' One of the two young men muttered sleepily, but the other opened his eyes wide, sat up and stared curiously at the quirky old man who kept kicking them. He was a strong lad, with very pale skin and eyes. 'Are you English? *It's forbidden! It's forbidden to sleep in the street!*' The boy looked too stunned to react. *'Are you German? Verboten!' Mr Zane did not know German, but managed to dig up a few words from his tired memory. 'Verboten in der Strasse!' He looked around for help: no one. 'Street! Go away! Go away! Raus!'*

Finally, the boy who'd sat up got out of his sleeping bag completely, staggering slightly and looking a little stunned, stretched widely and said something to his friend in a language that was neither English nor German. The other replied muttering, without opening his eyes, and even rolled over on to his side, turning his back to them. Mr Zane grew even angrier: he felt personally affronted by their thoughtlessness. He started shouting again, turning to the first, who at least acknowledged him; but then, having put his shoes on, he stood up, leant awkwardly against the wall, and accidentally kicked over one of the bottles, shattering it. At this, Mr Zane's fury reached its climax. He pointed to the glass shards and made it clear to the boy that he now had to collect them one by one. The young man obeyed, docile, bending down to pick up the pieces of glass and throwing them into one of the paper bags he had reopened (it contained two apple cores), while next to him the red-faced old man kept scolding him like he was a spoilt child. It took almost twenty minutes – it was almost eight o'clock and the sun was now high in the sky – before Mr Guido Zane managed to convince the two brats, so he called them, to pick up their clothes and their paper bags and leave. The laziest one, even taller, paler and heavier than the first, cursed in that peculiar language of theirs, while the other, milder one waved goodbye with a shy smile. The painter stood firm as they walked away and didn't move until he saw their two blond heads disappearing behind a bridge.

He took a few steps, but immediately stopped again: from behind the same bridge, the outline of a cruise ship emerged, advancing, guided by tugboats, towards the heart of the city. Still small at that distance, but rapidly growing in size as it approached, the ship was taller than the highest rooftops, churches or bell towers of the city: a real giant, a monster, precisely because of the falsely innocent and festive atmosphere it carried with it.

It had been a common sight for years now: many such ships sailed the canal every day, and Mr Guido Zane should have been used to it by now, like everyone else. Instead, every time, he would stand still and look in amazement at the ship, with its carnival designs and beehive balconies, and higher up, the crowd of passengers who thronged along the parapet, admiring Venice from above. He felt very small, and also a little scared, like a child; then he got annoyed with himself for being frightened. He couldn't help but imagine the ship hitting and destroying the white stone banks of the city, or even smashing the sublime façade of San Giorgio into bits; and the thought made his heart skip a beat.

Finally, he set off again: but now his mood was ruined. Even though the promenade of the Zattere was still almost deserted, even though the sky was bluer than ever and the lagoon lapped sparkling and festive in a thousand tiny waves that reflected the thousand rays of the sun, even though the façades of Palladio rose white and majestic from the waters, and so many fairy-tale houses lined up along the Giudecca bank, as though in a childish drawing, Mr Guido Zane no longer wished for any of this beauty. At the Gesuati, instead of continuing towards San Basilio as he did on mornings when the weather was good, he opted to go straight home, cutting through Viale di Sant'Agnese.

Until 20 or 30 years ago, there had been a succession of shops and cafés in that series of streets, alleyways and small squares that slipped, one after the other, on the tip of Dorsoduro. There was the bakery where Mr Zane had bought bread for most of his life; he had been sent there even as a kid, as it made the best rosette bread in the whole sestiere. The grocery where his wife Alberta often sent him to buy half a dozen eggs, usually just before dinner. The greengrocer, with its fabulous large yellow and blue striped awning, that he had painted so many times. He had felt a deep anguish when they replaced it with one of the usual dark red ones. There was the shop of the seamstress, a large, friendly woman with a Paduan accent, who pinned his pants, under the supervision of Alberta, before sewing the hems. The barber who had cut his hair for twenty years, Nane Rosada, with his motorbike magazines, who, if you let him, could talk for an hour about his bike skills. The shoemaker who, with his son, had fixed the shoes of his whole family – a couple of real Venetians who had neither motorbikes, nor cars, nor a driving licence between them, and loved nothing more than going out by boat to fish in the lagoon. There was also the Trattoria da Gino, a cheap inn always full of painters, and professors from the Art Academy, just a stone's throw away. How many times had Mr Guido Zane eaten there! He still remembered the feeling, between his fingers, of the curtain of plastic strips moving aside when you entered, back in the seventies. Plus a small hardware store, Marian, where he had always bought turpentine and white spirit. There was the wine-seller, Amedeo, with his large demijohns lined up at the counter. During the years of his marriage, Mr Zane would have eight bottles filled up every Friday, cabernet and merlot in the winter, custoza and white pinot in the summer. Once the bottles were filled Amedeo would offer him a complimentary glass, and told him the latest news. Then there was a haberdashery which he had only entered once, with his wife, because he couldn't believe that the buttons he wanted weren't available, only to be struck by the young and beautiful woman shopkeeper, with her round, snowy face like something out of a Veronese painting.

All those shopkeepers, who knew Mr Guido Zane well and greeted him when he passed by, flattered to serve a famous painter, had gone, one after the other. They had sold their shops at crazy prices, humble little shops that he had painted so many times with his easel on the street. They had retired somewhere to enjoy their unexpected wealth, and been replaced by shops for tourists: souvenir shops, commercial art galleries, so-called traditional restaurants. Nobody greeted him when he passed by, nobody knew him. To do the shopping, he had to go to a supermarket pretty far away, and to have his hair cut, even further. Shoemakers, haberdashery, hardware shop: all gone.

He reached home at a quarter past nine. 'I found two people sleeping,' he announced to Mrs Alina, even before greeting her. 'They were sleeping on the street, in sleeping bags.'

'Good morning, Mr Guido,' she smiled. 'How are you today?'

'Fine, thanks, but I was better earlier.' He sat down at the kitchen table, waiting to be served. 'Before I met those two on the street. Sleeping on the street, can you believe it? I've already had coffee.'

'Poor things, how uncomfortable. Can you imagine how hard that must have been?'

'No! That's not the point.'

'And how damp, on the ground. Enough to get sick.'

'No, no, they were young and strong. They weren't poor. They were tourists!' The supreme insult. 'Tourists too stingy to sleep in a hotel.'

Alina cut two slices of fresh bread, and spread them with jam, cherries and apricots, the way he liked. He was so fussy.

'Too poor, perhaps,' she suggested.

'If you are too poor to pay for a hotel room, you stay at home,' ruled Mr Zane.

She didn't want to contradict him. Her job, she knew, was to be patient and kind. She poured him a cup of milk, with just a drop of coffee; then she began to wash the dishes from the night before, while he, seated at the table, ate muttering to himself. When he had finished eating, he sat on his armchair in the living room, next to the French doors that overlooked the small square, with a book of Cézanne's reproductions in his hands. Usually, after his walk, he would start painting: he could still see quite well, but his arm soon got tired, and the sessions in front of the easel now lasted no more than an hour.

Today, however, he felt shaken, too moody to paint. He gave up. Instead, he decided to proceed with the task of rearranging his library: a project that had been progressing very slowly, because every time he started, he ended up being distracted by just two or three volumes, leafing through them from the first page to the last. Almost all of them were art books, thirty or forty years old, some even older, and turning their pages meant covering your fingers in dust. Meanwhile, Alina was tidying up the house, going back and forth between the rooms, making his bed, hanging out the laundry, dusting. That feminine presence, so sweet and discreet, had a calming effect on him. Finally, she sat down a short distance from him, and got busy sewing two buttons onto a shirt. 'What a beautiful day,' she said. 'It's really nice, with the windows wide open. You can hear the birds singing. And there's a light, fragrant breeze out.'

'It's Ca' Dario's wisteria,' he said gruffly.

'In my house, in Marghera, you can't keep the windows open, not even on a day like this,' Alina said. 'There's so much traffic, so much noise, you can't even imagine it, Mr Zane. There's a stench of cars, of smog! Forget the scent of wisteria!'

'And why can't I imagine it? Have I never been to Marghera?'

She was puzzled for a moment. 'Sure, but when? When was the last time?'

'Oh, I don't know. A couple of years ago, maybe.'

'Hmm,' she said doubtfully. 'To Mestre, yes; your daughter took you recently to Mestre to see the cardiologist, do you remember? The good one, Stefanini. In January.'

'Yup.'

'But what reason would you have to go to Marghera? In Marghera there are no doctors, no hospitals. There are only poor people, old factories, ugly houses, and shopping centres.'

'I don't want to see ugliness,' Mr Zane said firmly. 'I've seen enough in my life, and now that I'm old, I don't want to leave Venice any more than I have to, because the world beyond the bridge is too bad.'

'I know, I know, that's exactly what I was saying.'

'I could have left,' he continued. 'Many have left, for Rome, Paris. Why? I asked them. What's more beautiful than Venice? This city is a theatre, a stage. A precious casket. A dream. I'm not leaving.'

'Rome is beautiful too.'

'Sure. But in Rome, there is both the ugly and the beautiful, like anywhere. And I don't want to see the ugly. Not anymore. I've travelled. I've seen places. I've painted everywhere, in Rome, in Palermo, in Spain, in Greece. But now I'm old, I've had enough of the ugly. Do you know what Venice is? It is the only city in the world without ugliness. Here there is only beauty. And I want to stay here, in my casket, because I am old.'

They fell silent. He continued leafing through a book, recognising certain paintings that had captivated him so many years before, and among the pages, he found yellowed sheets with his notes on composition or colour. Then he raised his eyes and looked out: the seagulls strolling on the roofs, the two small art galleries opening for the day. The morning was indeed so bright it lit up the house – that sad home of a lonely old man – and lightened his bad mood with it. He would take another walk in the afternoon, perhaps. Of course, after ten, the city would be crowded: it was enough to simply look outside, to see couples, families and ever more numerous groups of visitors passing by uninterruptedly on their way to the Salute, the Dogana, and the Guggenheim. Irritated, but trying to remain calm and fend off discontent, the painter watched them from his balcony on the third floor. He was convinced that none of them cared in the least about those things: the basilica, built to thank the Madonna when the terrifying plague of the seventeenth century finally released its grip; the Dogana da Mar, a one-of-a-kind design by Benoni, with its triangular plan, its tower crowned by the golden ball, supported by two atlases, and above that the statue called Occasio, which is nothing more than Fortuna herself, turning to mark the direction of the wind while also representing the mutability of all our fortunes. What did they know? What did they care? At least tourists used to travel with a guidebook in their hand: they inquired, studied beforehand, even asked local Venetians interesting questions. Now they no longer asked a thing, and the guidebooks seemed to have disappeared, as have the maps, even the cameras: the only thing they had in their hands now were mobile phones. They simply didn't give a shit whether a church was Romanesque, Baroque or Gothic, they knew nothing and they understood nothing. They knew nothing of either Tiziano or Tintoretto – artists of whom Zane was so proud, so magnificent that he could feel tears welling up at the mere thought of what they'd painted. Tourists preferred the Guggenheim, a small collection of twentieth-century art, to the treasures of the Gallerie dell'Accademia, because they had become too ignorant and lazy to deal with a genuinely important collection. They enjoyed choosing souvenirs, pictures, coloured glass necklaces, without ever worrying that they were all cheap knock-offs made in China, or that, because of them, that prodigy that over the centuries had become the island of Murano, with its marvellous, inimitable glasses, was about to disappear. No, only one thing mattered to them: to reach the tip of the Dogana and take selfies with that fabulous scenery over their shoulders, and to then send their stupid photos around the world, to friends in Australia, India, Russia, Uruguay, Korea, Canada and the Emirates, to let them know they had been to

Venice. Thus, Mr Guido Zane mused, looking down on them with disgust before returning to plunge his nose into a volume on Cézanne.

Alina went to the kitchen and started cooking: every day she prepared lunch for him, a slice of meat or fish and a nice plate of boiled vegetables as prescribed by Dr Stefanini, with a minimum of salt and a teaspoon of extra virgin olive oil; for dinner, a pot of soup which he meticulously heated up at eight o'clock. They had lunch together, then Alina left and he went to bed for a nap.

While Mr Guido Zane was sinking into half-sleep, he could hear the buzz of the tourists through the closed window, which grew gradually louder until it seemed to completely clog the narrow streets which, for centuries, had been so quiet. He felt it as he fidgeted, dreaming. He saw his wife again, not as she had been in old age: slow, sluggish, often apathetic. No, he saw her as a young woman, beautiful and lively. Before meeting her, Mr Zane, who had just graduated from the Academy of Fine Arts, had taught drawing in the art college in Venice, dedicating only scraps of free time to his own work, painting in the evening under the electric light. Then, the wave of lively, artistic awakening also arrived in Venice, with an explosion of new galleries, new currents, and young artists. Santomaso and Vedova had arrived, with their amazing canvases, and later, in their wake, Tancredi Parmeggiani, Riccardo Licata, Cesco Magnolato, Amedeo Renzini: abstract art was consecrated, in Venice as it was everywhere else. Zane hadn't followed the fashion; he painted as he had always done, in a figurative style, but with a certain expressionist tone of his own that was quite original and that made his canvases distinctive and recognisable at first sight, as was the case, for example, with Renato Guttuso or Mino Maccari. The sixties, with its great, joyful cultural ferment, welcomed him with open arms, without criticising his attachment to the figurative: in that atmosphere of great cultural freedom, there was room enough for everyone. As soon as he set foot in the world of painters, Guido had met Alberta, who was a model. Love made him bolder. Almost by chance, without actually working for it too much, he found himself exhibiting his paintings and discovered an audience of admirers and buyers, so much so that the work was now occupying him day and night. Money was not lacking. In a brave act, he quit the college to devote himself full time to his art. As soon as Alberta graduated in Literature, they got married. Although she had been a model, she came from a good family: she too, like Guido, had been born and raised in Dorsoduro. Indeed, Alberta was from a bourgeois family: her father owned half a building on the Grand Canal and was a distinguished professor of archaeology, having travelled extensively. His wife had followed him on his travels and their daughter had benefitted from their trust and enjoyed her youth freely. But although known for staying up late at night, spending time in taverns, among artists and gallery owners, dancing, drinking and smoking, she was also a serious girl and Guido had been her first lover. Alberta taught for a couple of years, being a feminist and wishing for independence, but then her first child was born and, soon after, her second, a girl: in short, between one thing and another she quit teaching too. The money he made was enough; or at least it was until, in 1973, a third son unexpectedly arrived, and they were forced to look for a larger apartment, with at least three bedrooms, and a bright and quiet room where he could paint. Immediately they realised that it would not be an easy undertaking: finding such an apartment was pretty hard, because the houses in Venice had grown more and more expensive. True, there were the popular sestieri – Castello, Cannaregio, Giudecca – but Alberta did not want to live there and claimed that a painter could only live in Dorsoduro. Finally, she won, and they asked the help of both their families to buy this apartment in Campiello Barbaro, to everyone's satisfaction.

Those were the happy years that Mr Guido Zane was seeing again in his dream. They were blurry, confused images; fragments of dialogue; a look, a gesture, the noise of children, a caress on a young head of hair, illuminated by the sun, the feeling of walking by the sea, with bare feet sinking on the wet sand with a child in his arms; then a canvas full of colours, which was coming along well, and Alberta looking at it with him and saying something interesting and pleasant... but what? What had she said? And what was he painting?

When he woke up – which in the afternoon was a slow, difficult, almost painful process – he tried in vain to recapture something of those visions but they melted quickly away. Why was it so difficult for him to wake up from his nap – the old man was tormenting himself with this question – while at dawn he could leap out of bed, alert almost snappy? And why did a dull pain, deep in the heart, always accompany his awakening, as if something wanted to hold him back and prevent him from returning to the real world?

For more than an hour, he lay on the bed, without reason. 'I feel weak,' he said aloud, partly to himself, partly to Alberta, who, despite having died many years earlier, he sometimes felt hovering among the rooms of the apartment like a ghost. This was the old Alberta, however, the slow and plaintive one, with her hair dyed a brash yellow, nothing like the golden blonde of her youth, the one that annoyed him, like all ugly things.

'What were you trying to say in my dream? What were you going to say about my painting?' There was no reply. 'You don't remember, huh? You've lost your memory.'

'You are more foolish than me,' the ghost replied. In old age, she and Guido had spent most of the time arguing: they were harmless quarrels, teasing, squabbles; and when Alberta died, quite suddenly of a fulminating disease, he, for a moment, almost felt relief, for the silence and peace it brought him. But soon, as the months passed, he began to miss her dreadfully: he no longer had anyone to argue with. So now he addressed her as if she were still there, in those rooms; he addressed her mostly in grumbling tones, and in his imagination, he could hear her answer, equally annoyed.

'Here comes the first caravan,' he murmured to Alberta as he heard the first group of tourists under his windows every morning. 'Peace is over for today.' Passing by, visitors stopped to photograph the enchanting campiello. 'Here they go again,' the painter commented irritated, 'with their clicks and clacks.'

'But what clacks, Guido, what clicks?' retorted the ghost of Alberta. 'These days, photos are taken with phones and phones don't make that sound.'

Finally, he found the strength to get up. He went to the bathroom, rinsed his flabby face for a while with cold water, then returned to the living room. In the campiello, there was a great coming and going of visitors. Some had stopped to examine the works on display outside the two small galleries. They both sold rather cheap watercolours, displayed in plastic folders in book-shaped binders, and works of a certain level, paintings and sculptures, well arranged inside. They also sold Murano jewels and vases, in modern designs, as they proved quite popular.

Shortly after five, he saw Sandra. She came to see him almost every day, after work. By now, naturally – though to him so strange he couldn't fully understand it – his daughter was no longer young: she was fifty years old. Of his children, she was the only one left in Venice. The two boys lived far away; one in Milan, the other in Florence. They came to visit him, with their wives and children, at Christmas and in the summer. 'Daughters are every parent's treasure,' said Alina, who also had a daughter with her. 'Fortunately for you there's Sandra, otherwise how would you manage here all alone, with your children so far away?'

'I'm great,' Mr Guido Zane had snapped back, 'and I don't need anything.'

'I'm great,' he said to Sandra, as he opened the door for her, in response to her question.

'Good. Have you slept?'

'Too much,' he replied, annoyed. 'I slept too much. Who knows why I sleep so much.'

'Maybe because you get up too early in the morning. Would you like a cup of tea?' They drank some tea in the living room, chatting. He told her about the episode of the two young guys in sleeping bags at the Dogana; and while telling the story, he got nervous.

'Explain to me again why they annoyed you so much?' Sandra interjected, conciliatory.

'Annoyed me... annoyed...' the old man stammered, furious. 'Why do you think! Do you think people should sleep on the street like that? Do you think it should be allowed? Do you think it's decent?'

'But Dad, the world is now full of people sleeping on the street... You should see Milan... I was there last month, you remember, and right in front of the station, the moment you turn onto the avenue leading to the centre, it looks like a dormitory... Certainly not a nice way to present itself, as a city. Ultimately, you should think about those poor people who don't have a bed.'

Mr Zane was almost choking with anger. 'Do you want to compare Milan with Venice? This city is a jewel, a casket, a piece of art unique in the world! It is not like any other city! It's delicate. It's fragile. It must be handled with white cotton gloves, without leaving traces. It is a special case, deserving special regulations!'

'But for this very reason, Dad, precisely because it is so beautiful, isn't it right that everyone should be able to see it, even those who can't afford a hotel?'

'No! It's not fair at all! I would have liked to go to America myself! I would have loved to see Japan, the gardens of Kyoto! Yet I never went there, because I didn't have the money. We must be satisfied with the world we have.'

'On the other hand,' Sandra continued as if she hadn't heard him, 'sleeping under the stars, on a cold night... Think about it, Dad, nothing but water, stones and stars... It's also a nice thing to do, isn't it?'

'The stars? The stars what?' Seeing he was getting agitated, Sandra nodded and changed the subject. She went into the kitchen to see what Mrs Alina had left for dinner: a pot of risi e bisi,[3] and an omelette. She returned to the living room, satisfied. Finding her father still leaning out of the window, spying on tourists with a grim expression, she suggested they get some fresh air. 'Let's go for a walk,' she said. 'Let's go get an aperitif in Campo Santa Margherita.'

Mr Guido Zane looked at his daughter and smiled at her, with something very good in his smile. He could tell that Sandra was making an effort to cheer him up, despite having more than enough to do for her own family, each night, the moment she finished work. The aperitif in Santa Margherita had always been, for the painter, a familiar ritual, as relaxing and comfortable as a pair of worn slippers. After a long and lonely day spent painting, struggling with colours and shapes that didn't always obey him, with only Alberta for company on those occasions when she came into the studio to ask him, for example, if he preferred chicken or fish, unless you counted the boys who asked for money before running away slamming the door behind them, it was wonderful, yes, really wonderful, to go to Santa Margherita and find his friends there: painters, gallery owners, journalists and models. The cheerful little square, full of people whatever the weather, had the welcoming feel of a large drawing room. The square had always been the meeting place for students and intellectuals: there were the most beautiful, free-spirited girls, and the best of the youth. Now it had changed, although not that much: the students were still there, being part of the university area. It was he who had changed; he rarely met the few friends he had left in the world. When his walks took him to Santa Margherita, he would sit on a bench, quietly, looking around. No, it hadn't changed that much. Of course, the bars and restaurants were different now; they had invaded every corner and bore a more touristic signature. It was inevitable, even he understood that. But at least there weren't all those horrible Chinese souvenir shops that filled other parts of the city. 'It's a nice evening – there'll be a lot of people about,' Sandra warned him as they descended the stairs. 'Promise not to get nervous.'

'I promise.' Together they set out for the Accademia. Sandra held his arm and guided him safely through the crowds of people, who often stood in their way. Strangers passed by, loitering leisurely, ice cream in hand, moving in a zigzag manner from one shop window to another. The bright morning had given way to a quiet, golden light that dripped down from the rooftops like honey, around the long shadows of the afternoon. The swallows screeched above their heads, the air smelled of flowers, and everyone had gone out to enjoy the evening. After the Accademia, they found themselves trapped in a narrow street. Every now and then they took two steps forward, then they were forced to stop again. The multi-coloured swarm of visitors wound like a chain along the street, which had the shape of a narrowing funnel, and took a sharp turn before flowing into the San Trovaso Canal. There they had to huddle even closer to get onto the little bridge of the Maravegie, essential for getting to Santa Margherita. 'I told you there would be a lot of people,' Sandra said to him.

'It's a bit too much, you have to admit it.'

'It's because of the sharp bend,' Sandra said. 'Or Meravegie Bridge being so narrow. Have patience. Once we get over that we'll be flying.' But after they had been patient and crossed the bridge, they understood the reason for the traffic jam: there was work in progress on the next street, the pavement was scored with deep holes, which halved its width. The old man, forced to walk very slowly in the crowd, like someone in a religious procession, did not take long to burst. 'We are not in Mecca here!' A familiar refrain, for some time, in Sandra's ears, with which Mr Guido Zane often expressed his indignation and horror at certain dangerous gatherings of the crowd.

'Mecca! It's like Mecca! We can't go on like this,' he repeated angrily.

'I know it's not easy,' Sandra sighed. 'It requires patience. You pay a price for the privilege of living in such a beautiful place. Will you admit that you were lucky to be born in Venice, to spend your whole life here?'

'Why exactly? None of these people would like to live in Venice. None of them would swap that with me; none of them would give up their car. People should live with the choices they make!'

'But surely they have the right to visit? Venice belongs to the world, not just to Venetians.'

'But there isn't room for the whole world! We stand on our toes, literally!'

'All it would take is for them to put a limit on the numbers... you know they've been working on it for years.'

'I won't live to see it.'

'Maybe. But suffice it to say, there are many people who share your anxiety and your desire to protect the city. And they're working on it. Have faith.'

As they were talking, they reached Campo San Barnaba, at which point a muscular young man clearly in a hurry and desperate to escape the slow procession, bumped Mr Guido Zane so violently that the old man staggered and probably would have fallen, if Sandra hadn't been holding his arm so tightly.

'*Sorry!*' cried the young man, turning his head for a moment, and moving on quickly. A couple of people slowed down and asked Mr Zane, 'Are you OK? Did you hurt yourself?'

'Yes, he's OK, thank you,' Sandra answered for him.

'Rude youth,' commented an elderly lady, her eyelids tinged with turquoise, without stopping. Sandra led him to one side. 'Dad, are you OK? You didn't get hurt, right?'

'No, but what kind of... what kind of... scoundrel...' Mr Guido Zane went red again. 'Disgraceful...' He couldn't find a word adequate to his indignation.

'Yes, I know, but try not to get angry. Let's stay calm. The important thing is that you're not hurt.'

'... They are a disgrace...'

'Come on now, come on, it's late, it's nearly seven already, you know?' Without exchanging another word, they arrived in Campo Santa Margherita. In the centre of the square were the tables of the oldest café: they both loved it because it had remained almost the same over time. But the tables were all taken: and indeed there were many people standing, glass in hand, waiting for one to become available.

'We should have predicted this,' Sandra commented. 'We can go to one of those new bars. I can see a free table over there.' But by the time they arrived, the table had been taken.

'What shall we do? Do you want to go home? If you want, we can take the vaporetto. Or we can go through San Sebastiano and the Zattere, which will be longer but less crowded, I'm sure.'

Mr Zane protested: where was his sparkling prosecco? He had come here to get one. Going home with a dry mouth was not an option.

'Alright then. Let's grab a glass and go and have it there, on that bench.' Decision made, and with glasses of fresh wine in their hands, they headed for the bench. Unfortunately, when they got there it was no longer free. While Sandra had been ordering and paying for the prosecco at the bar, a Chinese family had spotted the bench: there were nine in total, adults and children, the latter sitting on the ground, cross-legged. In the centre, they erected a small gas stove and began pouring boiling water into bowls, full of freeze-dried thin spaghetti. Mr Guido Zane and his daughter stood watching them for a few moments, she with curiosity and interest, he absolutely stunned. Then Sandra took her father by the elbow, and gently guided him to another bench, equally occupied, but by some kids with spritz in their hands. They sat on the back of the bench, with their feet on the seat.

'Guys, please, would you be kind enough to let my father sit down?' she turned to them decisively. 'He's tired; he doesn't feel so good.' Two girls stood up, without saying a word, annoyed. The other two threw a distracted glance at the old man, and remained in their place, barely moving. Sandra got her father to sit and stood next to him. For a moment, she felt like the crowd was amassing, threateningly – an exaggeration, of course, a fantasy – ready to crush her father. But he sat upright, dignified, contemptuous, not to be intimidated. 'Now relax,' she told him. 'I need to call home for a moment to say I'll be late.' She took her mobile out of her bag and called her husband.

'They cook spaghetti in the middle of the street,' Mr Zane said as if Sandra wasn't busy in another conversation. 'This is what we've come to.'

Yet distant memories stirred within him. A tanned man in a white undershirt frying little fish in the corner of a campo, tipping them into a bag, his father paying and he, happy, walking beside him with the bag in his hand, shoving another fish into his mouth with every step. Even further back in time: a friendly, robust woman, kneading yellow flour cakes with raisins outside her shop, on a small table, smiling at the children who watched her, then passing them back to a colleague inside the pastry shop, to be baked. Why did she knead outside? Maybe it was summer and she was hot? In any case, the preparation and consumption of food outdoors, in Venice, had always been there...

Mr Guido Zane remembered so many stalls, so many vendors. Even there, right where he was sitting. Back then, when he was a boy, there were no benches or trees to shade them. Venice had never been an exclusive city: apart from Piazza San Marco and Riva degli Schiavoni, it had always been a rather working-class place. There were two second-run cinemas in Santa Margherita, the Moderno and the Vecio[4] (What was the latter's real name? Perhaps he'd never known). Kids in particular went there, himself among them, paying a few small coins. The Moderno stank. At the Vecio there was a stall that sold bovoleti and caragoi,[5] which the seller sprinkled with lemon. You ate them by extracting the mollusc with a pin brought from home; the shells were thrown by kids during the screening of the film.

'It is forbidden to eat outside, on a bench,' he told Sandra, who by now had ended the call. 'Anyway cooking outside, that must be forbidden!'

'I don't know, I don't think it is. But again, why are they annoying you?'

Mr Guido Zane did not answer. He was tired. He looked into his glass, then suddenly drained it. Then he got up, ready to go home, to his quiet and peaceful apartment that he was already feeling homesick for, and which seemed so far away. He accepted his daughter's proposal: taking the vaporetto from San Barnaba to Salute was a good idea. They arrived at the stop just at the right time, and got on smoothly. The vaporetto was crowded but the painter headed decisively towards the seats reserved for the disabled and the elderly, made a fat Dutch teenager stand up, and sat down satisfied, sighing loudly. All around him, apart from his daughter, were foreigners. There were some young French people, recognisable by their rather elegant linen clothes, but most were from further afield: Japanese, Brazilians, Canadians. Flip flops, shorts, caps and straw hats, although it wasn't quite summer yet. Mr Zane, by contrast, looked distinguished in his cool-lined overcoat.

Suddenly they heard a scream, right there on the vaporetto, the scream of a woman. There was a movement of general curiosity, as everyone craned their necks to try to see what was happening out on the bow. Had a woman fallen ill? Or had she dropped her phone into the water – something that happened almost every day. No, now everyone was looked further off, pointing to somewhere under Accademia Bridge which the vaporetto was approaching very slowly, as if it had slowed down. Then they started shouting and laughing. 'What happened?' Mr Zane asked Sandra, who was standing next to him. 'Nothing, Dad, don't worry...'

'Tell me. Tell me what you see,' he insisted. 'I can't see...' But just as he said this, craning his neck towards the window, he saw them: young people in the water, splashing around just a few metres from the vaporetto, cheerful, chatting with each other, like someone bathing in the sea. 'People in the canal!' he said in shock.

'Apparently they jumped off the bridge,' said Sandra, who seemed suddenly distressed. 'Such a dangerous thing, how stupid! They're probably drunk... And at this time of the day, with all the traffic in the canal... they could easily have hit a boat and killed themselves...'

'Killed themselves...' Mr Zane echoed.

'It's a common accident these days... there is this trend, you know, Dad, for diving into the Grand Canal... But it usually happens late at night... They shoot a video and then post it on social media.'

'But isn't it forbidden?' the father panted and snorted.

'Sure.'

'And why do they do it? The water's so foul!'

'Because they're young. Because they're drunk. Because there aren't any police officers.' As the vaporetto nudged slowly forward, the people around them cheered the bathers, waved at them, photographed them, filmed them.

'Someone will have called the police,' Sandra said. 'You'll see. They will come and give them a nice fine.'

'A nice fine,' repeated Mr Guido Zane. 'A nice fine will do it.' He spoke mechanically, in a weak voice, staring straight ahead, looking at nothing.

'Are you OK, Dad?'

'They foul up... they foul up this city... this casket. This precious casket.'

'Tomorrow you will read about it in the newspaper.'

'In the newspaper. Tomorrow morning.' Mr Zane felt he was being mysteriously dragged away, enveloped by a slow vertigo; he was moved by the realisation that the newspaper was now a distant object for him.

'To think that they dived right in front of us, in front of the nose of a vaporetto!' Sandra reflected aloud. 'What a stupid, provocative thing to do! I doubt they're even twenty years old.'

'Ugliness. I don't want to see ugliness.'

'Are you feeling ill, Dad?' Finally, he looked up; but he

seemed confused. He spoke to Alberta: 'They foul everything up. This precious casket, this theatre. The mud. The ugliness. They sleep, eat and drink sitting on the ground. Scoasse[6] everywhere! In this unique city!'

'Don't get upset,' Sandra pleaded. 'Nothing happened. Just silly kids. Nobody got hurt.'

'But diving... but...' Mr Guido Zane sank into memories. Seventy years earlier, when he was a child, even then there had been children and adolescents who dived into the canals. Not in the Grand Canal, of course; everyone knew that it was forbidden and dangerous, even though it was far less busy than today. But in the smaller canals, for sure. Yes. How many kids dived into them! They jumped in the canal fully clothed, pushing each other into the water, fighting, playing, even splashing those who passed by on the banks, especially girls. Not him, though, never. He was too polite, his mother had forbidden it, his father had explained it to him clearly: the water is dirty, no joke; you could catch typhus. So he watched instead, a little envious all the same.

How foolish young people are, yesterday as today... Curious to think that they hadn't changed that much, and Venice hadn't changed that much either... or had it? It was strange how his thoughts were tangling together. Those Chinese with their noodles... had they jumped into the canal from the deck of that cruise ship? Or was it those two tall, blond-haired young men from this morning? No, now he was sure of it; now he remembered with precision. It had been a certain Julius, taunted with the nickname Julius Caesar because he was so arrogant. He had been about twelve and already bearing a shadow of a moustache. It was he who had jumped into the canal, off Pugni Bridge, to a chorus of protests and good-natured curses from the boats passing by. A sultry day, with a dazzling white sky. Now he remembered everything, down to the smallest detail. He, Guido, younger than Julius Caesar, still a child, had stopped to watch from the bank, and had received plenty of splashes on his white shirt and shorts, worried about what his mum would say if his shirt got dirty, but also amused. More: he was full of admiration, excited, happy. He was experiencing the exact feeling of that hot day, water on his chest, stomach, that little thrill of desire, not so much to dive himself, but to experience the emotions, the adventure.

'... under the stars.' Sandra heard him murmur.

'I've always told you,' Alberta retorted. 'This obsession for the casket. Every time you came back from Rome, every time you came back from Milan, it was always the same story: how beautiful your casket was, how good life was in Venice, there was no such beautiful place in the world... The same old story! Meanwhile the others, your friends, were putting on exhibitions and becoming famous. Yes, I know that you've also exhibited in Rome and Milan, but small shows, minor galleries, because your head was always stuck here, in the casket, in this theatre.'

'Is it a crime to love your city?' Mr Guido Zane whispered, so softly that Sandra only saw his lips move.

'But cities must be experienced, touched, tasted. You should get hurt by, you should get fouled up by them. You have spent your life contemplating this city, painting it, but that's all. And now you're old you realise it and it's too late.'

At that moment, they arrived at the Salute stop, and the spiteful ghost of Alberta disappeared. Not without difficulty, Sandra helped her father to his feet; he seemed to have become heavier and much slower in his movements. She then accompanied him to the steps of the Salute, where she made him sit on one of them and, supporting him with her arm behind his shoulders, stared into his eyes and asked him: 'Dad, are you OK? What's going on with you?' He didn't hear her. For the first time in his life sitting on the stone, he gazed engrossed by the lights of the grand hotels as they came on, one after the other – the Gritti, the Bauer, the Monaco – and sparkled on the water.

Those first lights of the evening made him feel an immense longing: he felt his heart being torn between the love for that beauty that surrounded him and the doubt of having done something wrong. Twilight swirled with possibilities, memories, regrets.

He remembered walking on rooftops, as a boy, slipping on unsteady tiles; he remembered climbing a pine in Sant'Elena park, his hands sticky with sap, and nostalgia made his heart beat in his throat. He wanted to paint Venice once again, he wanted – unthinkable! – to dive into its waters and sleep on its stones. 'A painter can only live in Dorsoduro,' he murmured, but again the daughter heard no sound.

His clear eyes reflected an expression more uncertain than ever; indeed, after a minute, they seemed utterly expressionless to Sandra. Did he recognise her? She spoke louder. 'Dad, I'll call an ambulance, OK?' she asked, still undecided.

Finally, he looked at her: and it was the last good smile of Mr Guido Zane. It lasted only a moment, and only Sandra saw it, even though others were approaching; then the old painter closed his eyes, and never saw Venice again.

Notes

1. A Venetian word indicating a block of stone carved in order to make it an element of the pavement. The word corresponds to the Italian 'boulder' and was prevalent in Italy until the nineteenth century.

2. Tiny squares. Venice has only one 'piazza' (large square), that of San Marco, and many 'campi' (small squares, from the Italian word for 'field'). A 'campiello' is even smaller.

3. A peas and rice dish from Veneto.

4. The old one.

5. Two types of sea snail.

6. A Venetian word for rubbish.

A Farewell to Venice

Michele Catozzi

1

THE NEWS SLAPPED HIM in the face like a cold borìn[1] blast.

It didn't really surprise him; there had been rumours about it for a while. In fact, it annoyed him. The plan to move the headquarters to the mainland had been on the table for at least thirty years, but it never got beyond that: a recurring rumour, good for having a laugh with colleagues, over a coffee or a spritz in a bar.

This time, however, thanks to an unlikely alignment in the intentions of at least half a dozen local, provincial and ministerial administrations, it was starting to look pretty damn serious. *Il Gazzettino*[2] was unequivocal:

NEW POLICE HQ IN MESTRE WITHIN
THREE YEARS
City Council, Metropolitan City, Interior Ministry
and State Property Office have signed a
memorandum of understanding

The new building will be constructed in Marghera
on the site of a former school, and will bring

together the immigration offices and police stations of Marghera and Mestre. Additionally, the offices of the Patrol Operations, Criminal Division (aka Flying Squad), General Investigation and Special Branch (DIGOS), as well as other local police offices will all be relocated there, from the city centre [...] The restructure will bring consistent savings and the first to profit from these will be the taxpayers[...]

The office of the Flying Squad... the taxpayers... Nicola Aldani needed to talk with the police commissioner right away. He slammed the newspaper down so hard Bepi got worried.

'What's going on, Inspector?' the bartender asked, ceasing, for a moment, the twisting motion with which he was polishing the dented steel bar.

The policeman didn't answer, shaking his head.

His first thought was to call his friend Danieli, *Il Gazzettino*'s crime correspondent.

'Hey, Inspector,' the voice on the other end said, 'what's going on?'

'You're the second person to ask me that in as many minutes.'

'Did you get out on the wrong side of bed, or something?'

'No, just read the papers.'

'So it's the HQ thing that's got on your nose.'

'We have to meet.'

'Let's say lunch?'

Aldani left the bar with a vague wave of the hand.

The night before, a light storm had cleared away the clouds and humidity. The crisp, May morning air, with its brackish scent mixed with the aroma of hidden gardens in bloom, put him in the mood for a leisurely stroll, not that now was the time for leisurely strolls.

He lingered along the canal side, where a couple of small,

battered tables – the three-legged metallic ones you can't get anymore – balanced precariously on the masegni and Istrian stone that lined the bank. Up ahead, the murky waters of the Grand Canal churned with the swell maintained, beyond reason, by the procession of vaporetti, barges, mototopi,[3] taxis and motorboats, that also contributed to the background hum he was all too familiar with.

He was headed for Scalzi Bridge on foot. Travelling upstream, like a salmon against a river of tourists without even attempting to dodge them, if anything almost barging into them deliberately with a certain disgraceful pleasure which masked, he well knew, a childish attempt to blame them for this latest disaster.

Cascades of people continued to pour into the large square in front of Santa Lucia Station. You could always spot first-time tourists from the way they stopped, mouths agape, to admire the city, their eyes drawn instantly to the copper-green dome of San Simeon Piccolo that shattered into a mosaic of shards strewn across the waters of the Canalasso.[4] In doing so, these first-timers got in the way of the more experienced ones, equipped with backpacks or trolley-cases, fanning out without hesitation along the more beaten routes towards the Rialto and San Marco, or Piazzale Roma. Others stampeded towards the ACTV vaporetto pontoons in front of the station, where, despite the early hour, queues were already getting longer and longer. What a mess. And this was just May. The city was tottering on the edge of an abyss, and everyone turned a blind eye to it.

The tourists who dragged along big, old-fashioned suitcases attracted swarms of Sinhalese porters angling for work. Native Venetian porters had long been ousted, with the consent of the Municipality which, unable to confront the long-standing unlicensed activity, had to relent and endorse the state of things. It wasn't all plain sailing, every now and then scuffles broke out, mainly with taxi drivers, who were, by contrast, all still strictly 'locals'. As he passed, Aldani overheard one such heated exchange, and was about to alert the foot patrol, when the argument was suddenly nipped in the bud. Just as well, he didn't want any more trouble right now.

He kept walking along the Fondamenta Santa Lucia towards Constitution Bridge, which everyone called Calatrava Bridge after the architect who 'donated' it to the city. A heavy present, which condemned the Municipality to undertake expensive, ongoing maintenance work thanks to its chronic flaws. Like, for example, the glass steps that should have been its crowning glory but instead became a nightmare for pedestrians who – come ice or rain – ended up stuffing the hospital's casualty ward. Maybe they would replace that glass soon. For once, perhaps, the city's thousand-year-old wisdom might prevail over the genius of its 'star architects'.

From the top of the bridge that crossed the Grand Canal at the zirada,[5] you could see the police headquarters building, a few hundred metres away. On one side, the building – on which the square markings of the former Santa Chiara Monastery were still visible – overlooked the canal; while on the other, it practically backed into the end of Liberty Bridge. It had a double entrance, from the canal and the street: boats on one side, cars on the other. A perfect metaphor for this damn city. But for how long?

His stomach knotted and he pushed on towards Piazzale Roma and the headquarters.

2

The aftermath of a difficult investigation awaited him in the office: piles of paperwork to fill in and reports to write, lest the deputy prosecutor get upset. Magistrate Privieri was clever, but perhaps too much of a stickler for procedure, boring as it was obligatory. But the forms would have to wait, now he had more important things to do.

'Good morning, boss!', a police officer greeted him with candid enthusiasm.

'Good morning my ass, Manin.'

'What's going on?'

Aldani answered with a grunt, as usual. There was a bad atmosphere, and the moment a blundering colleague appeared at the door, Manin vanished, taking the colleague with him.

In the offices of the Flying Squad, it was going to be a long, tiring day's work.

'I'm sorry for barging in, but it's a matter of the utmost urgency.'

'What's going on, Aldani? Any news about the Sbardella case?'

'No, Commissioner, this is not about a current investigation.'

'Fine. I actually thought that matter was over.'

'Indeed.'

'Well, then? Aldani, come on, don't make me ask you twice!'

'Is it true that HQ is being relocated to Mestre?'

'So that's what this is about?'

'And is it true that the Flying Squad will end up in Mestre too?'

'Where HQ goes, the Flying Squad goes; it seems obvious to me.'

'But what do you think about it?'

'Well, after years of vacillation, we finally seem to have some solidity on the issue.'

'Spare me the bureaucratic language, sir.' He immediately regretted this line, bordering as it was on insolence, but it was too late to do anything about it.

The commissioner sighed. 'Listen, Aldani, we've known each other a long time. Face facts. It seems a perfectly rational decision if we're to improve the service for the taxpayer…'

'Getting rid of Headquarters won't improve anything!'

His superior looked at him in silence for quite a while. 'Tell me the truth, Aldani, isn't it rather that you have grown fond of this office and don't want to leave the city centre?

The echo of the question bounced around inside his head, but he couldn't answer. Damn the commissioner! The inspector stood there like a stuffed owl, incapable of forming a complete sentence in reply. Partly because there wasn't actually much to say.

3

Aldani remained in his office, willfully ignoring phone calls, simply staring at the waters of the Grand Canal, relentlessly furrowed by the vaporetti buzzing around the piers of Piazzale Roma. He could hear the muffled noise of traffic from Liberty Bridge. Every now and then a sepolina[6] – as the police affectionately called the old patrol boats, owing to their remarkable gracelessness – left, sirens blaring between two wings of water, turning onto the Rio della Scomenzera that led straight to the Marittima,[7] then on to the Canale della Giudecca, the quickest way to San Marco. This view calmed his soul, and the idea of moving to Marghera, into a nondescript, albeit modern office, made him feel irrationally claustrophobic.

The meeting with the commissioner had been a disaster. Too bad, he'd hoped for better. He didn't even consider talking to Schiavon, the Flying Squad's chief superintendent and Aldani's direct superior – as the inspector was a member of one of the five sections that made up the division: 'homicides, sex crimes and crimes against the person'. It would have been a waste of time. To talk to the prefect[8] was out of the question, that bureaucrat wouldn't even receive him. What's more the commissioner would take it amiss that he'd gone over his head. Schiavon too, come to think of it. The politicians, likewise, were off-limits. He couldn't stand them anyway, and they couldn't stand him. A long time ago, the mayor took issue with a couple of 'summons' he'd sent him, not to mention the regional president, who avoided Aldani like the plague. And the Region didn't even have anything to do with the 'move'. The District, that is to say the Metropolitan City, were the ones behind it, and annoyingly the president of that was also, by sheer coincidence, the mayor himself…

Aldani felt powerless.

It was at this moment that a flash of instinct showed him clearly, if only for a few seconds, what to do. A bookie would have given him twenty to one against, but he decided to try anyway. He left the office like a hurricane.

'Boss…' Manin called after him.

'I'll talk to you later!' the inspector snapped, leaving a worried grimace on the officer's face. It wasn't Aldani's intention, but he'd explain later.

Venice's Public Prosecutor's Office – located, along with all the judges' offices, in the so-called Citadel of Justice – was just a few minutes on foot from HQ. One of the few sensible projects pulled off by public administrators, the Citadel stood on the far side of Piazzale Roma, on the site of a former tobacco factory.

He crossed the street right in front of the military armoured vehicle, parked as usual in the middle of the road, surrounded by concrete blocks; a feeble deterrent against international terrorism. The heavy traffic of cars and buses seemed to welcome his recklessness with noisy hoots.

Constructed alongside Liberty Bridge in 1933, Piazzale Roma still performed its osmotic function of integrating land and water. Aldani skirted it, from the side of the municipal car park, that glorious multi-storey edifice of the same era, navigating between the tables of a pizzeria and the usual bewildered crowd of first-time tourists trying to process this unexpected expanse in the context of a floating city: a huge, asphalted area, polluted as badly as any metropolis (if not worse), surrounded by haphazard buildings and global-brand kiosks whose main use was to sell rubber boots at exorbitant prices, in case of high tide.

The entrance to the Citadel of Justice was marked by a very modern brown, wedge-shaped building, so out of place it was almost pleasant. After identifying himself at the reception desk, Aldani marched straight to the offices of the deputies. He knocked gently.

'Good morning, Prosecutor.'

'What's going on, Aldani?' the prosecutor, Luisa Privieri, asked in a surprised tone. 'Don't tell me there are new developments in the Sbardella case.'

He sighed, hesitating.

The woman stared at him for a moment: 'No, I guess not. There's a storm brewing, I see.'

'I'm sorry for bothering you, but…'

'If you're here, I'm guessing it must be something urgent that you can't put off. Am I right?'

Aldani took the crack, with all its sarcasm, and chose not to rise to it. 'Have you read the papers?'

The woman nodded with a grimace, urging him to come to the point.

'The relocation of HQ.'

'Ah! So, this is what's so urgent!' she said with palpable relief.

'It's a serious matter, Prosecutor,' he objected, this time, piqued.

'Come on, Aldani, the relocation seems reasonable, doesn't it?'

'I'm not buying it. Relocating HQ would be deeply symbolic, it would be a declaration of impotence, like admitting that Venice is not enough of a city to need its own. It would be like abandoning it!'

'Let's not get carried away. And anyway, Venice *is* different to the other cities.'

'I know!'

Privieri made no further comment. Standing up, she grabbed a folder and placed it on a trolley overflowing with papers. 'I know how fond of it you are, but even with your office in Marghera, you'll be back in Venice soon enough, don't you think?'

'It won't be the same.'

The woman shook her head. 'It's personal for you, isn't it?'

Aldani offered nothing but petty silence.

'Even a bit selfish, don't you think', the prosecutor added, grabbing another folder. 'What do you propose to do?' she asked, finally.

'I'll do everything I can to prevent this.'

'Is that all?'

'I'm serious. And you need to help me.'

4

The journey from Piazzale Roma to Campo San Polo usually took about fifteen minutes at a Venetian pace – that fast stride of someone who knows where they're going without the need for the yellow signs – RIALTO, SAN MARCO, PIAZZALE ROMA, ACCADEMIA – scattered around the streets and squares heaving with 'foresti', as Venetians call foreigners; the pace of someone who doesn't need to stop, puzzled, at major crossroads where arrows point in all directions, let alone ask for directions, which, by the way, is pointless because Venetians will only ever point to the horizon in front of them and give the same, hopeful answer: *Straight on!*

The Venetian pace was hampered by continually having to slalom around dawdling tourists congesting the streets, and having to shout at them to keep right, while resisting the urge to step on their stupid toes. Aldani had once seen the hilarious sight of a girl who, having flattened the feet of a tourist standing in her way with her trolley-case, delivered an impeccable British 'sorry', only to let off, a few metres away, a string of curses in Venetian dialect, as colourful as they were unrepeatable. Ah, the eternal love-hate relationship between Venetians and tourists!

The sun was beginning to burn in the square, so the inspector was grateful to slip inside the cool atrium of Palazzo Corner-Mocenigo, the provincial and regional headquarters of the Financial Police, whose spotless façade overlooked Campo San Polo, while the other side of that imposing building dominated the eponymous canal. Land and water, in perfect balance.

'Long time no see!' Captain Colucci exclaimed, impeccable in his uniform as always, and clasping Aldani's shoulders firmly.

'You're right, we should meet more often.'

'What brings you here?'

Aldani spotted a newspaper on the desk. He approached, pointing at the offending article.

'Yes, yes, I just read it. What do you think?'

'Bad, really bad!' was his straight and decisive answer.

'OK, have a seat,' his colleague said. 'I presume you have something to say on the matter.'

Aldani sat down. 'How are your relations with the higher-ups?'

'We get on, why?' Colucci asked a little suspiciously.

'And with your fellow Carabinieri?[9] You get on well with the military, right?'

5

It was almost lunchtime and he didn't want to be late for his meeting.

He gave up the idea of taking a scenic route via the Rialto, and instead made for the traghetto stop connecting the Pescheria[10] with Campo Santa Sofia, on the opposite side of the Grand Canal. He inhaled the strong smell of fish made all the stronger by the warm weather. Every time he crossed the old covered market, his heart ached at the sight of the few surviving fishmongers who resisted the fall in customers and fought against those amateurs working in urban planning.

The Rialto was the centre of old Venice, the heart of all trade in the Serenissima Republic. Now, just a shadow of its former self, the sword of Damocles hangs over its head, as it faces being converted into nothing but a tourist destination, as has already happened to many of the historic shops in the area, now converted into trendy bars as part of the growing movida.[11] The same perverse mechanism currently loomed over the Arsenale. He didn't dare imagine what would happen if the Navy, which still garrisoned a sizeable portion of the ancient shipyards, decided to leave.

The gondolon – longer and wider than a traditional gondola – was about to leave the dock. He jumped aboard throwing a coin on the side of the boat, as Venetians do, planning to stand up throughout the crossing. It wasn't that easy, considering that the two gondoliers, one at the bow and one in the stern, were doing their best to navigate the swell, unscathed. A shiny, mahogany motorboat, one of those that came with their own driver, and only hired by tourists with the fattest wallets – two of whom were sat at the rear enjoying the sun – skimmed past the ferry in defiance of the speed limit and strict regulations against the swell that was literally destroying the city. The two rowers launched into a volley of curses which spared nobody, not even the dead relatives of the motorboat driver, and hung over the water for a long time.

Aldani could hardly stand up. If he had been aboard his little Toni, he would have ordered Officer Vitiello to turn his siren on and set off in hot pursuit. Even though he knew those kinds of infractions fell well outside of his duties as homicide section officer, it would at least console him to bust the balls of the arrogant driver and to ruin the wealthy tourists' day out.

6

'You're late,' Danieli addressed him curtly, waiting impatiently in front of a diner in a side street in Cannaregio, not far from the Jewish Ghetto.

'I know, I went to see Colucci…'

'…to complain about the HQ thing,' Danieli finished the sentence. 'Let me tell you something, Inspector, you really are a pain in the ass.'

'Shall we go in?'

Dino's was a place from another era, catapulted right out of the seventies. On the other hand, finding a good diner in town was impossible. It was an old-fashioned place for old-fashioned Venetians. Tourists didn't even try to enter: the only words in Italian were TAVOLA CALDA DA DINO and the notice PIATTI DEL GIORNO stamped on the top of the small slate hung outside. Everything else was written in pure Venetian dialect, unintelligible to foresti, like the menu (Risi e suche – Bigoi in salsa – Sarde in saor co poenta – Folpi consi) written with chalk in impeccable handwriting.

Inside, the air was saturated with thick cooking smells, a hazy mixture of miscellaneous flavours hinting at that day's menu, making everyone's mouth water. They sat at a yellow Formica table, dating back at least half a century.

Dino, the owner, materialised right away. He and his wife struggled more and more each day to keep the business going, given their old age. Aldani didn't fail to notice Dino's expression, more disconsolate than ever.

After a short negotiation, Danieli got the best of the fish options: folpi consi,[12] apparently lighter than the other dishes, together with half a litre of the house Tocai.

The journalist was staring at his friend with interest.

'What are you looking at?'

'I'm worried for you, Inspector. I've never seen you so indifferent when faced with the question of what to eat.'

'What the fuck are you talking about, Danieli?'

'Relax, I'm just teasing you.'

'Come on, just get to the point. We need to stop this nonsense.'

'Why are you speaking in the plural?'

'Because you're going to help me.'

Danieli laughed. 'And how might I do that, may I ask?'

'You are a journalist. You could…'

'Listen, Inspector, I guess you are thinking about a petition or something. I can tell you now it won't be enough. You have to involve the big shots, win them over, only then will you have any hope.'

'I don't know any big shots.'

'Indeed.'

'It doesn't matter; I'll give it a try anyway.'

'Bravo, and then what?'

Aldani looked at his friend for a long time with an expression that must have seemed imploring.

'Fine, you could do with not looking like a fool. I'll give you a hand. I'll probably regret it, but you know I'd do anything for my favourite officer!'

'Won't the editor give you a hard time?'

'Who, Gavelli? No, no, even if he has a habit of siding with the establishment, he remains a good journalist who cares about his newspaper, and in these lean – very lean – years, you'll see he'll appreciate the mess that comes out of this; after all, more mess means more readers and more copies sold.'

'If you say so.'

'Trust me, I'll take care of it.'

They drained the last few sips of Tocai, toasting each other with renewed optimism.

Aldani had barely touched his food, while Danieli, glancing worriedly at the inspector from behind a dish laden with chopped octopus seasoned with oil, salt, pepper, lemon, and especially sliced celery, couldn't resist, in fact, he even ate his friend's portion.

The officer looked at his mobile to check the time, and only then remembered he had put his phone on silent. There were ten unanswered calls, mainly from the police headquarters switchboard, a couple from Manin and one from Schiavon. What the hell did the chief want from him?

At that very moment, almost as if he'd been summoned, he received a call from Detective Manin.

'There you are, Inspector, finally!' he snapped. 'Chief Schiavon has been looking for you high and low.'

'And what does he want?'

'I have no idea, but he seemed pretty angry.'

'So what else is new? Listen, find a motorboat and send it to pick me up in front of the Scuola della Misericordia. Make it quick.'

They ordered a coffee, then Aldani accompanied the journalist outside. 'Thanks, you're a good friend,' he said before saying goodbye.

Then he headed back in to tie up a loose end. 'Now tell me, Dino, what's going on?'

The man hesitated. 'Well, the thing is that Maria and I are old, Commander...'

'I know, and your son is a prat and doesn't help you. You've told me dozens of times.'

'We need to consider the future. Our future and the future of Giacometto. We have received an offer to sell the business. From a company. Foresti.'

'And what do they want to do to the place? I'm assuming these people don't really give a damn about the diner.'

'Commander, once they buy it, they can do whatever they want. We are old,' Dino concluded with a desolate expression on his face. 'But I heard your conversation,' he said changing the subject. 'I think you are right, something must be done.'

Aldani looked at him, slightly taken aback.

7

When the Toni arrived, almost gliding in, leaving behind a seething wake of murky water and a procession of boats crashing against the paline[13] and piers, Aldani was still mulling over old Dino's words. Without a generational handover, a part of the city as he knew it was destined to disappear, swept away by the wave of cheap bars for tourists that were plaguing Venice. There was no stopping it.

'Here I am, boss!' Officer Vitiello exclaimed, with his typical chronic cheerfulness and lingering Rome accent that years of being stationed in the city had failed to eradicate.

'Take a look behind you,' Aldani suggested.

The officer turned around to witness the disarray he had created along the narrow Rio della Misericordia, then spread his arms and lifted his lower lip. 'Detective Marin said it was super urgent so I...'

'Not to this degree,' Aldani cut him short jumping into the cockpit next to where Vitiello stood downcast in front of the wheel. 'Come on, let's go.'

The Toni was one of several government boats issued to the police, and represented something of an anomaly: devoid of official colours, being simply painted white, and recently restored and upgraded, it was the only one that could bear a 'name' and not just a serial number.

The motorboat pulled away from the bank and turned into the busy Rio di Noale. From there it reached the Grand Canal and turned right towards the railway station and Santa Chiara, negotiating all the comings and goings of vaporetti, motorboats and mototopi.

'Boss, I was told they want to move HQ.'

'True.'

'That's not good. If I can help with something, I'm at your disposal.'

'Thanks Vitiello. For now, I'd be content if we just got a move on,' he said with a fatherly smile.

'Of course, boss!'

As usual, the officer obeyed the order to the letter and pushed down the throttle to make the engine roar. The Toni surged forward and the inspector had to grab the railing to stay on his feet. At some point he'd have to give Vitiello a lecture about this, but not now, not with the knowing expression that the officer had on his face. What's more Aldani was having too much fun darting along the Grand Canal in between the curses of all the marineri,[14] fresh air lashing his face.

Moments like these, he just loved his job.

8

Vitiello brought the Toni alongside one of the piers where other government motorboats and sepolinas were moored, and the inspector jumped off. A sign saying QUESTURA[15] (and below it, in a smaller font, POLICE, to underline, as if it were necessary, the city's ever outward-looking focus) hung over the entranceway for the former monastery. Aldani popped his head through the door of the Sea Division, the office that oversaw the distribution of police boats, for a customary greeting to the boys, then continued under the porticoed cloister, where the colonnade lined the edge of a wide inner court, now used as parking space for police and civilian cars.

He bounded up the stairs to the Flying Squad's offices and presented himself at Schiavon's office.

'Here I am, Chief. What's going on?' he asked slightly out of breath. He was convinced that such a detail would help suggest an air of diligence, which wouldn't do him harm.

'At last! Where the fuck have you been?'

'I was consolidating my informal network of contacts in the city,' the inspector answered, in all seriousness.

Schiavon gave him a sidelong glance: 'Are you taking the piss?'

'Absolutely not, Chief.'

The other man sighed. 'What's all this about you being against the relocation to Mestre? Are you off your head? Why didn't you talk to me first?'

'I've never said that...'

'Yes, you did. Or you led people to understand that, at least. And that's the same.'

The commissioner must have let it slip. Aldani tried to explain himself, summoning up all his oratory skills and drawing from his albeit limited rhetorical repertoire. Without success. Schiavon, the straightforward, sometimes rude man that he was, drew his conclusions.

'I get it, you don't want to go to work on the mainland.'

'Chief, it's a bit more complicated than that.'

'Yes, yes, it may be more complicated, but the end result is the same.'

Aldani sighed.

'Listen, I genuinely know where you're coming from, but you have to realise it's a lost battle.'

'You know where I'm coming from?'

'In a manner of speaking. Anyway, forget it.'

9

When detective Manin knocked on the door, the inspector was busy in a vain attempt at reducing his backlog. That said, typing on the keyboard one finger at a time, driven by an almost non-existent enthusiasm, his productivity faltered and the pile of paperwork grew to an almost dangerous height.

'What do you want?' he asked, more gruffly than necessary.

'We heard, boss.'

'Who's we?'

'The boys and me.'

A long silence followed.

'We wanted to tell you that we feel the same as you. And if there is anything we can do…'

10

That afternoon Aldani got very little done; he was lost in his thoughts. It was time to go home. The one in Mestre, where Anna and the kids were waiting for him. Something, however, was gnawing at him.

'Anna, I'm staying here this evening.'

'A new investigation?'

'No.'

'No one got killed today?'

'You're not funny.'

'I didn't mean to be. It's about the relocation, isn't it?'

Aldani didn't answer.

'I guessed you'd get paranoid about it.'

'You reckon?'

'I know you too well. Fine, I'll just leave you at your holy of holies.'

'OK. Kiss the kids for me.'

He gathered his things and went out.

As he approached Campo San Leonardo he remembered he didn't have anything to eat back at his place. That said, he didn't actually live in Venice anymore, his family had moved to a spacious apartment in Mestre, and the place in Ghetto Novissimo barely had any furniture, just a small kitchen. He considered whether to eat out or buy something from his usual biavarol – the grocery shop run by the Mion brothers. He opted for the latter.

It was an old-fashioned place that had survived – god knows how – the sea change in intended use that transformed so many local shops into attractions aimed at tourists: butchers had become boutiques selling fake leather products; bakeries had turned into shops selling carnival masks or Made-in-China 'Murano' glass; ironmongers had morphed into American-style fast-food restaurants; confectioners had been repurposed as shoddy goods emporiums; and groceries had turned into pizzeria/chips/candy/chocolate franchises. You were spoilt for choice.

The Mion brothers were old, and didn't have any heirs – like déjà-vu, these situations were always more recurrent in cities where the resident population was falling relentlessly while tourist rentals were proliferating exponentially, more or less illicitly. In their grocery, Aldani breathed the same stale air he had done as a kid, saturated with the smell of local preserves and exotic canned food, salami and cold pork, mackerel in oil, stockfish hanging on the wall, pickled olives, smoked herrings and dried beans. It was the same air he had breathed in Mestre, although in those parts they called it 'casolin'.[16]

With a lump in his throat, he bought a couple of loaves of rosetta bread and a hundred grams of soppressa.[17] He thought about it for a moment, and eventually added a bottle of prosecco. He greeted the brothers warmly, then headed home, thinking it wouldn't be long before the Mion brothers were pulling down their shutters for the last time.

The inspector reached his apartment on the third floor of the building. After preparing the sandwiches and opening the bottle, he headed up to the altana, setting the dish and a full glass on a small table, before taking a seat on a battered wicker chair. He sighed with satisfaction as he enjoyed the lukewarm air that smelled of wisteria, sage and rosemary. It had been a rough day, but finally he was there, in his favourite corner, the one that Anna, teasingly called his 'holy of holies', an apt epithet in truth.

The altana, in Venice, was a small sheet of wood perched above certain rooftops, a platform suspended above the tiles, plainly fenced, offering a privileged vantage point over the city in all directions: in the background, on one side, the lagoon, the mainland and, on clear days, the Alps, and on the other side, the Lido's strip of land and the Adriatic. An aerial platform exposed to winds and bad weather, but above all, the sun. There was never a single patch of shade on the altana. It was a corner of peace where you could let thoughts wander, a place where the noises of the city became muffled and its problems seemed distant.

The sun had already set and the darkness fallen, cloaking Venice in all its nocturnal wonder, a mantle of light and shade, darkness and reflections in the water.

He would never have confessed it but that altana, with its wisteria climbing up from the square below, and Anna's aromatic potted plants, was the reason he had never really broken free of the house, even after moving the family to the mainland. He, who was born in Mestre and had spent many years there, somehow felt Venetian to the bone and the altana was...

All of a sudden, as if he had never really thought about it, he realised that if his department were moved to the new HQ in Marghera, the opportunities to stay overnight, right here, would be slashed.

Aldani sighed and decided to go back inside. At that moment, Danieli called.

'What do you think about reaching out to some of the neighbourhood committees and civic groups?' the journalist asked point-blank.

'I'm not really familiar with...'

'I am though. Don't worry, you're in good hands.'

11

Three weeks later

It had taken a while to work out the plan. In the end, he had passed on all the relevant information to Danieli and was happy to just sit and wait for the big day. Aldani entered the bar at a marching pace.

'Good morning, Inspector, have you seen the paper?' Bepi asked with an enormous smile.

Aldani didn't answer. 'May I?' he asked an elderly client

eagerly reading the obituary page. The old man didn't seem too pleased, but Aldani didn't wait for an answer, snatching *Il Gazzettino* from him, flattening it out on the bar under the benevolent gaze of Bepi.

Danieli had managed to wrangle four pages' worth of articles and interviews from his editor, as well as the six column-wide title on the front page.

VENICE IS RISING UP: EVERYONE IS AGAINST THE POLICE HEADQUARTERS MOVE

A petition signed by almost 13,000 people and the support from key, senior figures is set to seriously challenge the proposals, already approved regarding the convergence of offices in mainland Marghera.

The proposed relocation of Venice's headquarters to yet-to-be-built new premises of Marghera, in a few years' time, has crashed unexpectedly against a wall of complaints from across the city. As evidenced by the numerous interviews and testimonies featured in these pages, the uprising sees the Public Prosecutor's Office at the front line, something undoubtedly unusual. The PPO clashed with the commissioner and prefect, not so much about the construction of the new headquarters in Marghera designed to unite the police stations of Marghera and Mestre with the Immigration Office of Marghera, something it 'considered necessary and rational', but rather the relocation of Venice's Police Headquarters and the Flying Squad to Marghera. According to one of those criticising the move, Deputy Prosecutor Luisa Privieri, 'It would be a huge mistake, a sign of weakness which organised crime – that has long attempted in to infiltrate the economic and social fabric of the city – will exploit to take even further control.' A similar line is taken by Brigadier General Luchetti, head of the Financial Police Regional Command, who argues it would be 'a completely inappropriate and glaring signal of withdrawal from the territory.' As does Colonel Adinolfi, head of the Carabinieri Provincial Command, who foretells 'unavoidable and unforeseeable repercussions for the security of citizens.' In short, it seems that nobody is questioning the rationale of having joint premises – to consolidate the current offices on the mainland seems perfectly reasonable – but the verdict is unanimous: the Venetian Police Headquarters have to remain where they are.

Even amongst Police HQ staff, the dissenters seem to be increasing in number by the hour and seem to include not only dozens of police officers but also almost the entire staff of the Flying Squad and the DIGOS, and even the highest authorities such as the chief of the Flying Squad, Superintendent Schiavon, who has allowed himself to speak quite publicly on the matter. Not to mention Commissioner De Girolami who, albeit lukewarm on the issue at first, now seems to have jumped unequivocally to the other side – although nothing official has been said so far – endorsing the stance of the majority of his men.

The prefect, acting as the long hand of the Minister of Interior, when questioned on the matter, took refuge in an understandable *no comment*. Similarly, the city's political leaders didn't want to intervene: the Governor of the Region and the mayor (as well as President of the District, sincerest apologies, *'Metropolitan City'*). They are preferring to remain silent, no doubt hoping the whole thing will blow over in time.

The story doesn't stop with the authorities. The uprising includes ordinary citizens and traders. Among the most active small businesses collecting signatures for the petition have been Bepi's Bar in Fondamenta San Simeon, Dino's diner at Misericordia, and Gastronomia Mion − the delicatessen in San Leonardo. In recent days they have become the command centres for the rebellion and have been able to recruit scores of other businesses. Suffice it to say that, at time of printing, they have collected in the region of 12,597 signatures, an achievement − unbelievable only a week ago − owed in part to the support of various Venetian civic neighbourhood committees, a fragmented, heterogeneous constellation of activists from different backgrounds and stances, which in a spirit of rediscovered unity has enthusiastically joined the initiative attaching to it a great symbolic importance and raising it as a flag of the citizen resistance.

This writer doesn't recall, in his many years covering the city, a revolt so broad-based, so united, so fervent, so grounded and, let me say it, so justified.

Indeed, because there are no economic reasons nor cost rationalisations to defend it, the preservation of the Police Headquarters in Venice is a duty, a mark of respect towards an already beleaguered city that has been vilified for years by decisions that put the interests of the few before those of the whole community.

Now it's up to our readers, and all citizens, to pass judgement on this issue and, hopefully, participate in its resolution.

Claudio Danieli

Aldani remained dumbfounded, staring at his friend's article.

'Nice, huh?' Bepi asked, smiling.

'Uh-huh.'

'Good job, Commander!'

'It's all thanks to you,' he insisted with an ostentatious gesture of the hand, and he really meant it. He grabbed the phone and dialled a number.

'Impressive. You've outdone yourself.'

'Thanks, Inspector.'

'Steeped in civil fervour!'

'Even journalists have a soul, you know.'

'You cretin. But where's it all going to end?'

'I don't know; we've done everything we can now. Cross your fingers and hope for a domino effect.'

12

One week later

And domino it was. A freak wave that rose and rose until it overwhelmed everything.

The surge overwhelmed any tipping point, beyond which everyone thought it better to be carried along with the current and not resist. All of a sudden, everyone (or almost everyone) found themselves on the same side.

The upper echelons, including the Minister of the Interior – who thus put an end to the controversy – agreed that while it was reasonable to consolidate the mainland police stations into a single location, it would have been foolish, if not counterproductive, to remove the Police Headquarters from Venice itself. A healthy dose of the classic, Italian trasformismo,[18] but this time Aldani could forgive it.

The only person who was disappointed and held out to

the very end was the mayor, alias the President of the so-called Metropolitan City who, on the contrary, thanks to his well-known fondness for the mainland, didn't stomach the turn of the events too well. Not that this was a problem, it seemed a done deal by that point and, if everything went as smoothly as Aldani was hoping, HQ would be staying right where it was. As would, more importantly, his altana. But that was a pretty selfish and unbecoming thought, he realised, for which, out of guilt, he immediately repented.

The inspector knocked on the door and opened it slowly. 'Commissioner, I want to thank you for what you have done,' he said in an uncharacteristically calm tone.

'Dear Aldani, I didn't do anything at all, it's all thanks to you.' The commissioner still couldn't commit himself, that was clear. But the inspector didn't buy it.

'Sure, sure, of course... Thank you, anyway, for doing nothing.'

It was ten in the morning on a bright, sunny day. Venice was waiting for him outside, more splendid than ever. He decided to take a long break and go and thank all the people that helped him, one by one, inside and outside HQ. There were so many.

Notes

1. A Venetian word for a wind coming in from the north-by-northwest.

2. A local daily newspaper.

3. Typical Venetian lagoon transport boats.

4. What Venetians call the Grand Canal.

5. A Venetian word meaning turning point or bend.

6. Little cuttlefish.

7. The Venetian harbour.

8. The prefect is a representative of the territorial government and metropolitan cities who responds to the Ministry of the Interior.

9. The national gendarmerie of Italy who primarily carry out domestic policing duties, one of Italy's main law enforcement agencies, alongside the state police (Polizia di Stato) and financial police (Guardia di Finanza).

10. The Fish market area.

11. Nightlife.

12. Boiled musky octopus salad.

13. Mooring poles.

14. Sailors.

15. Police Headquarters.

16. A Mestre dialect word for delicatessen, or grocery; while the Venetian dialect word for it, would be 'biavarol'.

17. A typical, Venetian spiced salami.

18. Flip-flopping, or political U-turns.

Carmen

Elisabetta Baldisserotto

THE NEIGHBOURS CALL HER 'the singer' and her first name is Carmen, what a coincidence.

She turns in late each night, and around 1am can still be heard singing softly as she rinses out the washing.

In the morning, she lets herself go to louder trills while she hangs out the clothes. To her neighbours, she is a familiar sight, in her wooden clogs and loose, black and grey check shirt, as she oils the pulley, cleans the clotheslines with a sponge, hangs the washing, only to later pull it all back in and hangs some more.

She stands in the middle of the street busying herself with a basin full of wet laundry on the doorstep next to the basket of coloured clothes pegs. She inhales the scent of the tepid tablecloth. Holding it by the corners, she stretches it out so it hangs perfectly and, when it's dry, folds it back carefully.

The sun never reaches this street, but there are enough draughts to make the ropes groan and the washing flap. Her son's jeans are so pretty and well-cleaned that people steal them. It's happened more than once. Someone turns into the street, sees Fabio's jeans, puts them on and leaves their own dirty old trousers on the ground.

Then Carmen screams. She screams so that the whole

neighbourhood can hear her. Because it's painful. So much effort was put into washing and hanging them stretched and straight. Besides, Carmen doesn't have the money to buy a new pair. Her husband only does off-the-books jobs and in the evening, when he comes home after first dropping in to all the local osterie,[1] his eyes are bright and his face flushed.

Carmen screams and asks if anyone saw who did it. The kids playing football nod: someone was buttoning up Fabio's trousers close to the clothesline. A guy from Santa Marta with rotten teeth, who staggers around before collapsing asleep – 'That's who did it,' the sweaty, out-of-breath kids say. Mrs Gina appears at the window and tells her about a spate of thefts that happened twenty years ago.

On hearing this Carmen hangs the washing inside. She keeps her fold-up clothes-horse in the doorway next to the umbrella stand and hangs the shirts to dry on the coat hooks on the wall.

The apartment on the ground floor is small, but smells of fresh laundry. There are clothes almost everywhere, just washed or taken out of the closet to get some air.

How nice is the sound of the washing machine when it spins clothes around in its warm belly! It's like the sound of a boat riding over waves, the bow lifted so high that it falls down again with a slap.

How nice, when the tiny red light flicks off and Carmen can open its door and thrust her hands into the damp, defenceless wool amazed to still be alive. Clean pants, good as new, socks not harming anyone with their smell anymore.

When Carmen goes grocery shopping she observes other people's laundries hung out to dry. This is how she learned to put an extra peg at the bottom of the trouser thigh to keep them straight so they don't twist around the rope, and how to hang socks in pairs, pants in order of size, then t-shirts, towels, table linen, sheets and pillowcases. Each item hanging by its edge to dry evenly.

If you hang the washing properly, it's easier to iron it and for some items, like napkins or pants, one quick ironing is enough.

Some women hate to iron, they say it's conducive to negative thoughts, because it's not a dynamic activity, one that relieves tension and leaves you tired but light-hearted. Yet, it does make Carmen want to sing. She saved up to buy herself a steam iron. Because it feels like a way of treating clothes better, even cheap ones. Steam makes fabrics pliant like hair washed with conditioner. When the job's done, shirts, which are the hardest to iron, look brand new, just taken out of the cellophane. Carmen doesn't fold them nor store them in the drawer, she hangs them on the walls instead of paintings.

How horrible when it rains all day and looks like it will never end! Carmen feels deprived of her primary function: to wash clothes. But when it's the world outside's turn to be washed, she can't do her washing, because then it wouldn't dry. And when clothes become damp with the humidity it's as if someone has sweated in them.

Today there's an incessant drizzle, and Carmen moves anxiously round the rooms, not knowing what to do with herself. Her husband hasn't got up, since it's raining. She looks at him snoring with his mouth wide open: he always leaves those white saliva stains on the pillow.

She tidies up Fabio's stuff: boots left in the middle of the room, crumpled t-shirts, balled up jeans. Every now and then she peeps out the window to see if the sky is cleaning up. It's raining so heavily that Mrs Gina's patch of lawn has become a muddy puddle. She doesn't like Fabio's friends. They spend entire mornings at Zattere, sitting on a bench drinking beer. They shout and argue, while the girls quarrel. They ask for money from passersby and then go to the supermarket for a refill. If it would just stop raining!

At 1am, when it stops raining, Carmen hand-washes her laundry, to keep the noise down. She plunges her hands in the soapy water and starts to sing sotto voce. Then she rinses the washing out and goes outside to hang it. The air starts to turn again, the sky shaking off the clouds.

Somehow, all of a sudden, her wedding ring slips off her finger. She hears it rolling on the pavement, clinking. She follows it till the centre of Campo San Sebastiano, bending over to see it better.

The little square is deserted; only the pink houses and the apse of the church cast shadows. Carmen keeps searching.

Two hours later she's still there, staring at the ground, when the dogs pass by and bark at her.

Note

1. A traditional Venetian tavern.

Beautiful Venice

Gianfranco Bettin

I HAD WORKED FOR a few days on the beach, between Malamocco and Alberoni, on that thin strip of land that separates the Adriatic Sea from the lagoon. A raging storm, which went on all night, had first eroded the beach and then covered it with residual sand, as well as all kinds of debris: a forest of timber, bushes, uprooted trees, dead branches, evergreens, together with a firmament of starfish and shells.

An extraordinary cleaning operation had been necessary. It consisted of manually collecting and piling up all this material which would then be removed with mechanical vehicles by a specialist contractor. I had earned a few hundred euros, struggling quite a bit in the cold autumn wind.

I didn't go to Venice often and, in truth, I didn't like to go. I was born there, but we had left when I was only three. Our house, owned by an ecclesiastical charity that from time immemorial had rented out places at low prices to working-class families, had recently been converted, along with the rest of the building, into a guesthouse for tourists.

I remembered almost nothing of the little time I spent in Venice. And despite growing up so close to it – we had only gone to live on the mainland, just across the trans-lagoon

93

bridge – it felt like another planet: a city of asphalt, of fast, chaotic, cars, high-tension pylons, factories, shipyards, giant cranes, and technology. Venice was just a silhouette, a postcard, a recurring escape – the Redentore,[1] the Carnival, a few cultural events, the Lido and Alberoni beaches.

It was also the nostalgia my parents felt for it. They couldn't stand this distorted planet of which I, on the contrary, felt a natural inhabitant. My father had a limp and struggled to walk due to an accident he suffered while working at the docks. The accident had left him disabled and forced him into early retirement. He quickly gave up revisiting old places and old friends. In Venice, with his injured leg, he moved slowly and painfully. A heart attack took him from us too soon. The broken heart of the uprooted, I always thought, swearing that no melancholic yearning for something that didn't exist anymore would ever take hold of me.

Where we ended up living became the only place I had, a new city, almost without a name, but it was enough for me. It was still Venice but it was the *other* Venice, the one that only Venetians (and not all those) recognise as such. Friends, streets, schools, my world, my time.

Since the age of eighteen, before I even finished high school, I have worked here and there. I enrolled at the biology faculty at Padua for a while. After a year, I switched to environmental sciences at Mestre, the modern branch of Ca' Foscari University.

In the meantime, to pay for my studies and support myself, I joined the cleaning branch of a multi-service cooperative, although I did a little bit of everything, adapting to any job. Usually, we sorted through rubbish at the city dump, picking out the good pieces to send for recycling, leaving the rest for disposal; or we fed things onto conveyor belts leading to the machines that separated glass from paper, plastic from glass, or the other way around. We had an eye for what had to be saved and what had to be eliminated.

It was not uncommon for us to work in different places, in particular on the lagoon or by the sea. In such environments, it wasn't always possible to do everything mechanically and even specialised firms often had to resort to manual intervention. Not just to clean the beaches after winter storms. The opposite could be the case: even the calm of the hot season sometimes made manual intervention necessary. The summer before the storm, for example, we had to intervene several times.

That spring, as it happened, saw a lot of rain. Between April and June, there had been repeated thunderstorms, as well as slow and heavy rainfall and rapid downpours, persistently.

Rainwater, surging through rivers and canals, and pouring over banks, had brought into the lagoon, from the hinterland, civil waste and chemical fertilisers full of substances used to intensively fertilise the flatlands. Summer came and, because of the heatwave, we witnessed an abnormal blooming of algae. Green meadows, vivid and rotten in colour, covered vast stretches of the lagoon for several days. By July, at the end of its life-cycle, the algae had died and was floating on the surface, exuding the smell of rotten eggs, the odour of putrescence, specifically hydrogen sulphide. Yet, the annoying smell that the wind brought to the city was only the prelude of a much greater, imminent disaster.

In the hottest days of July, the parts of the lagoon where the phenomenon was most acute became deadly traps for all forms of life, especially fish, which were exterminated by hydrogen sulphide, a ruthless, amphibious angel of death. To cope with the situation, an extraordinary collection of algae was undertaken. Specialist machinery, boats called 'pelicans' with huge mouths and skips in the rear, were deployed to chew up all that greenish hair, scalped from the bottom, or suck up all that bile-coloured foam into which the algae had transformed. Manual labour also proved to be useful. We collected what the mechanical pelicans failed to collect, fishing out algae with nets, as we followed behind in small flat-bottomed boats suitable for even the shallowest parts.

We had been busy with this for a week but we knew it wasn't going to end there. Towards the end of July, an exhausting, relentless heat had brought the lagoon to a standstill. It was suffocating. All currents had ceased as if the water had fallen into a deep coma. The areas where the algae had first proliferated and then died and putrefied, absorbing all the remaining oxygen in the process, were now churning with mullets, sea bass, anguanella, paganelli, sole, passarini, gò, bream and even crabs, fighting for breath at the surface before finally floating, belly up, their little corpses swaying sadly in the still water, so light they bobbed with every ripple. The death of fish, caught in the lethal trap that was the hydrogen sulphide, was not unheard of in the heat of summer, but had been exceptional that year. A swarm of dead, silver bodies now laid where the algae had lay rotten before. The water was so still partly because there was no wind and partly because the progressive silting up of the canals, unexcavated for some time now, had blocked its flow, preventing it from reaching out into the thick texture of the lagoon. The tide, however, even at such times of extremity, naturally carried on ebbing and flowing every six hours, up and down – *sie ore la cala, sie ore la cresse,* as they say in Venice, almost like a philosophy. The tide was coming in from the sea, entering through the harbour mouths and pushing up to the innermost corners of the basin, sweeping those patches of death along with it. From there, as it ebbed back, it dragged with it, towards the city, all of those little, scaly, glistening carcasses.

They arrived in Venice in their thousands on a Saturday evening, gathering at the Fondamente Nuove and then entering the historic city centre through several of the larger canals. And this wasn't just any weekend either, it was Redentore, the largest Venetian festival, when tens of thousands of people would gather on boats in the San Marco basin or on the banks between Schiavoni, the Zattere and the Giudecca to watch the foghi, the famous fireworks. During the night, most people didn't notice what was quietly entering the city. The next morning, however, everyone was able to witness a very different spectacle. By that point, the fish had floated into the Grand Canal.

It was easy to recognise the most recently deceased fish as they were like delicacies for the seagulls and cormorants that, like spoilt gourmets, discarded the less fresh ones.

They called us at dawn from the Municipality. Armed with the usual nets and aboard the usual boats, we spent Sunday and Monday competing with the seagulls for the dead fish. The seagulls, at first, resisted our attacks, fearlessly fighting for their meal, but then they retreated, clearly replete.

I was in the middle of arguing with a ginormous herring gull, when I spotted, in amongst the dead fish and wobbling algae, a wooden board, about a metre long and thirty centimetres wide, torn at the sides, and of a colour that must have originally been red, with blue writing on it. It looked like a piece of a sign. Who knows how it ended up in the water.

'he Beautiful Ve' it read. The Beautiful Venice, or Venezia, could be guessed by adding what must have been the missing letters. A souvenir shop, perhaps. Or maybe a little café. It floated among the fish corpses like a little raft adrift.

Beautiful? I wondered. I smiled at the irony. And also the revenge. An evocative message from a city that had lost us, let us go, perhaps even chased us away, that had abandoned my mother and father to their disorientation, to lie in that hot soup of dead currents. A beauty eroded, cast away.

I took a picture of that artefact, the wandering sign, while the rest of the waste-collecting boat ignored it and continued its sorting of carcasses and algae.

The autumn storm forced us to carry out a more tiring, purely manual intervention. Bending, digging, pushing, brushing, carrying the rubbish by hand or with crates or wheelbarrows, our work boots sinking into the heavy, waterlogged sand, stumbling over branches, animal carcasses, all kinds of furniture, toys and bric-a-brac thrown by the Adriatic Sea onto the shore. The Adriatic has always been a treacherous sea that grows all the more frightening in the storm. Being shrewd and experienced navigators, the Venetians always feared it, taking every precaution whenever they ventured onto it. Happier rather to live protected in the heart of the great lagoon, aside from the odd exceptional tide.

After the collection – and after having piled up all the natural waste on one part of the beach and all the rest on another, separated by type (glass, plastic, cans, etc.) – it would be the turn of the specialist machines and other, more skilled workers. They would try to rebuild the beach, putting in new sand and then leaving it to the wind and time to consolidate the shoreline, shape dunes and grow new vegetation.

I was taking a break, sitting on a log thrown up onto the shore. Bundled up tight in my anorak, I was munching on an almond bar, when my gaze fell on something red a couple of metres away, among the brushwood, algae and wet sand.

A bird was hovering above it; indeed the way it moved so cautiously around it caught my attention from the corner of my eye. It was, I then realised, an uncommon specimen of godwit, the Limosa limosa. A prudent, quick-witted animal. Before it flew away, which was almost immediately, I was able to briefly admire its long, slender legs, its thin orange and black beak, and its grey-brown winter plumage (in summer, by contrast, the male's feathers turn brick red).

I followed it as it flew, low, towards the crashing waves, as if it wanted to dive into them. But then it veered upwards last minute, skimming the tops of the waves and climbing up in the wind, performing a kind of somersault to head back inland and zip across the dunes that had resisted the deluge on the ridge that overlooked the few metres of beach still remaining. Then it disappeared. Looking back to where I'd first spotted it – or rather, where the Limosa limosa had spotted me! – I noticed some blue marks against a reddish background, which was, as it turned out, an abandoned wooden board, semi-invisible, half-covered as it was with algae and dark sand.

The marks looked like drawings, or symbols until I saw that, partly obscured by dirt and encrustations, they were actually letters: *B tif V*.

Look who's back again, I thought.

The Beautiful Venice.

The sign must have reached the sea slowly, in the intervening months, carried by the lagoon's currents, and the sea must have then returned it, throwing it onto the beach, with the storm.

Sie ore la cala, sie ore la cresse – the water that ebbs and flows every six hours, that comes and goes, cleans the lagoon, in the endless, vital game of the ecosystem.

The beauty of Venice.

Yes, the mosaics. The golden light of San Marco. And the strong, quiet order of its architecture. The triumph of colour in San Rocco and so many other places. Evenings on the canals and the sight of stars above the domes, above the roofs of houses standing steadfast in the water. All the things that everyone knows and admires. All the things we left behind when we moved away, together with the world my parents once lived in, and their parents, and the generations before them, from tide to tide, from century to century. Since time immemorial.

Here is the beauty, instead.

I didn't think about much else in the days that followed.

There is a different beauty. Different from the one we all see, the splendour in the foreground. There is another beauty, more vital and visceral as well as painful. It is hidden in all that rotting algae, in all those silvery fish writhing in agony in the rocking water in bad summers. It is in the violence of the sea, in the storms on the beach. In the movement of the tides, in the ebbing and flowing water as it carries away and brings back everything, just like the flow of human history, but with a wilder, clearer sincerity. It is in the long, slow cycle that winds its way into the city, into our work, into the incessant labour of nature: whatever calculation is and the measure of our relationship with it; whatever instinct is, and that feeling of belonging to it. Everything is primordial and everything is mathematical in Venice, where the tide reigns, governed by the stars.

Is there anywhere else like this, that deserves to be called home? A home we built, in a universe that, continuously, builds, destroys and rebuilds itself. Can there be a more authentic beauty?

Sitting on the trunk, I retrieved from the photos stored on my phone the one I had taken the summer before, during the algae harvest.

Yes, it was the same wooden board, the same drifting sign.

Then I had Googled it.

As it happens, there had indeed once been a small

souvenir shop called *The Beautiful Venice*. It wasn't clear where it was, somewhere in the general vicinity of the borough of Cannaregio. There was also a photo, online, in which you could see a small room, with a window displaying objects in wood and fabric, decorated with Venetian and lagoon motifs.

Another photo showed a young, smiling girl with a pearl nose-ring and tribal tattoos on her bare arms standing in the shop entrance, with an elderly lady who resembled her, perhaps her mother, with a stern but elegant expression. They were images that dated back three or four years, then no other clues attached to them.

I picked up that faded-red board, freeing it from the sand and brushwood that half enveloped it, and carried it home. I dried and cleaned it, recovering the surviving inscription: *he beautiful Ve*. I didn't quite know what to do with it, so for the time being I left it there, in the storeroom where I'd cleaned it, in the basement of the council block where I lived with my mother. Our apartment in Mestre, at the end of San Marco Avenue, in a neighbourhood built back then to accommodate families from Venice where the streets were oriented to point in the exact direction of the San Marco's bell tower. We live on the fifth floor and from my room I can very clearly make out the skyline of the historic city, beyond the water mirror of the lagoon.

I have been wandering around Venice for weeks, whenever I get a moment, looking for that little shop, on the off chance it still exists, even with a different name or address. I've also been going back through the places that once belonged to my family, even if I'm not sure of the exact address. I go there alone.

My father is dead. Perhaps he would not have come with me, his leg would have prevented him from coming, or perhaps his reluctance, his bitterness would.

My mother, on the other hand, is still full of energy. She knows many women in the neighbourhood, attends the parish meetings, is active in an association of elderly women who organise charitable activities – collecting and redistributing used clothes, mainly, but also trips.

One day, knowing she hadn't been to Venice for decades, I asked her if she would come there with me for a walk. She had never returned, but I had the impression that she didn't even look at it from the window. Her window and the one in the living room, looked northeast, towards the mountains, and I often saw her looking that way, on the balcony, silently smoking a cigarette. But I've never seen her look out of my window, towards Venice.

She looked at me curiously when I made this invitation. She didn't say anything at first, then eventually she just said, 'Fine.' She got dressed and we left. Once in Venice, my plan was to wander aimlessly, but she remembered every street perfectly. Thus, we easily arrived in front of our old house.

She hadn't been there for decades; she'd only returned a few times in the very early days after we'd been driven out. I, on the other hand, had never been back.

Casa Soggiorno was written on a brass plaque by the front door, and below was the name of the owner. It was mid-November, low season, but there were still people coming and going, dragging trolley-cases or with backpacks on their shoulders. Families, teens, elderly couples.

My mother looked at the facade, the windows on the second floor that had been ours.

'Let's go,' she said.

We returned home, slowly, like an exhausted ebbing tide.

The next day, I showed her the photo on my phone of the shop and the two women, the girl and the one who might have been her mother.

I asked her if it reminded her of something, a place, a clue.

She looked at the photo for a long time, as if sinking into it.

'I don't know who she is,' she added, pointing at the girl. 'But this one' – she said smiling and clearly moved – 'is called Rosa. Rosa Marcon, daughter of Teresa and Giacometto. She has, or had, three sisters, Marina, Maria and Monica, and a brother, Seba. Sebastiano. They had a sewing shop, near the Misericordia.'

'Could it be this place?' I asked, pointing to the little shop in the photo.

'It could be... But it's hard to tell. And this sign…,' she murmured.

'Maybe it's the new name, maybe the shop was passed on to her daughter?'

'She could be Rosa's daughter, sure. She does look like her. We were very close friends, even with her sisters.'

Then she fell silent, with a hint of a smile.

I pointed again to the sign that could be seen in the photo. 'I found it,' I told her.

'What? You found what?'

'This. The sign. I'll tell you where I found it. Wait for a moment, I'll go down to the basement.'

I ran downstairs, jumping like a kid. Once down, I took the sign and, holding it under my arm, I ran up again.

'Come, I said to my mother,' taking her by the hand.

We went to my room and I put the wooden sign between the computer and a pile of books on my table under the window.

I told her about the original writing, what it meant. And about the agonising tides of summer and the furious ones of autumn. I told her how they had passed this find between them. She remained silent. She just stood there, looking at that red table, thinking, crying and smiling, looking at its incomplete writing, but also beyond: beyond the sign, beyond the window, beyond the end of the avenue and the lagoon, beyond the mirror of green and blue water, to finally look once more at the city where she was born.

'It's so beautiful,' she said.

Note

1. The Festa del Redentore (Feast of the Most Holy Redeemer) is an event held in Venice on the third Sunday of July where fireworks play an important role, giving thanks for the end of the terrible plague of 1576, which killed 50,000 people.

Atmospheric Conditions

Enrico Palandri

1

AFTER RUNNING TO CATCH one of the rare vaporettos that cross the Giudecca Canal at night, I walked slowly, along the Fondamenta delle Zitelle looking at the stars. It was a late summer night, the breeze blowing over the lagoon was stroking my hair and face, piercing the heat. In the relief of those cool, invisible caresses, I found once again the friendly hand of solitude, ready to pick me up even from small failures. I watched the vaporetto crossing the canal, and then looked to the sky again.

I imagined the silence, and the thoughts hiding among the dark shades of the night: the waves, the clouds, the shadows. The sky was empty and, if gravity were not holding me tight to the ground, the speed of the earth's rotation or other movements would have thrown me into the void, alone, to an infinite distance. I imagined not dying, never being able to die again, resisting hunger, thirst, needs. I imagined the end of feet and hands, the end of breath; the eyes, on the other hand, remained open to stare at that fall in which even great meteorites, planets, entire galaxies become nothing but bodies scattered in the void, fragments of an explosion thrown randomly in different directions. I imagined I no longer had a mouth to scream, or any way of even feeling fear. My ears too remained open, forced to listen to silence, on both sides.

I would no longer be sleepy or feel tired, there would no longer be any distraction to spare my conscience: the vigil would have neither rest nor end.

Following the imaginary itinerary of that fall through the sky, for a moment I thought I had finally reached my absence; then I noticed a movement in the water, a lapping of the waves breaking against the stone steps of the fondamenta.[1] I looked for something, I didn't know what exactly, but something, among the sounds. I returned my eyes to the stars, thin wisps of air flowed into my nostrils. I held my breath in search of what I had lost, ready for the interstellar journey that I had sensed was about to start, but was now, in fact, over; the need for some fresh air suddenly forced me to inhale again, the way pain forces you to scream. Anxiety and pain too had disappeared, like gusts of wind in the air or small waves in the sea; nothing had happened, I had imagined all of it.

I arrived home when it was almost morning; dawn was rising over the roofs to the east spreading over the entire surface of the sky; in that still very light blue, the dark silhouettes of the buildings in Campo San Polo looked like giants sleeping around an extinguished fire. I dragged a chair to the window overlooking the little square and sat waiting for the morning, listening to its noises: verandas opening and ageless women looking out to greet the day after their rest. Someone was hurrying along the paved street at the end of the square, the echo of their footsteps lost between the sides of the street and the singing of birds, some of which were already flocking across the sky, high and distant. Ducks, probably. Others, meanwhile – swallows and swifts – flew lower performing splendid solitary spirals. Others still, glided sleepily, at ease in the air, letting themselves fall from the clouds almost down to the roofs before regaining altitude with a single stroke of the wing. Coming to Venice had been the right choice, it was so beautiful. It was a pity it was so hot during the day. Only at night was it possible to stroll around the city. I got into bed and lingered a while, letting my eyes wander beyond the window, among the clouds and electric cables stretched across the square, until the city was awake and the noise of the day, sweet and continuous as a lullaby, sent me to sleep.

I woke up a few hours later. My thoughts, still dry, were already rising one by one from the bed, arranging themselves in order for the day. I would work on the interminable translation I had taken on as a guaranteed source of income for a few months; then I would call the landlady to complain about a damp patch on the ceiling; I would even buy a newspaper and maybe think about proposing an article to Tommaso. It was sunny outside, a lively day, full of people and activity; the loud voices of children and the murmuring of adults rose from the square into my room. I squinted, as if by doing so I could shut the noise out. I also wanted to reflect, examine the questions I was avoiding the night before, but shame kept me locked in a silence where my difficulties remained unspoken. I had come to Venice to start a new chapter. It was all very beautiful, I kept repeating to myself, and that was something at least, even if I said it just to distract myself from the bewilderment of those first few months. I didn't know anyone in town yet. Everything was new. Fearing my own interrogation, I turned over in the sheets in search of one last remnant of sleep, or at least a clearer determination. I would wait a little longer.

Life was thus floating away, just like a breath into the closed sky of a room. I didn't want to ask myself if it was worth it. I was waiting, something would happen eventually and before I knew it, it was evening again. I hadn't looked at the blue of the sky, I hadn't really slept, I had made little progress with the translation which, instead, seemed to have grown in length, nor had I proposed anything new to Tommaso. I gathered up my cigarettes and jacket and hurried out. The apartment door, the stairs, the main door, the street, the walls, the closed wells, the still water and eventually the sky. Far away, among the stars, I would have been fine there, in the freezing cold and perfect darkness. It was living among others that caused me problems. I was breathing slowly, not knowing where my nocturnal wandering would take me, then I cleared my throat and asked someone for a match.

2

I had sat to smoke another cigarette on the steps of a house behind the Tolentini, shortly after midnight; I listened to the footsteps of people coming and going along the fondamenta which the walled steps led down to, each briefly invading the space between the two walls. A boy and a girl were whispering and their voices, despite them reminding each other to speak quietly, were very clear.

'Kiss me again, Nina, then tell me to leave.'

'Come on, come up. I swear it's not risky – my parents are heavy sleepers.'

'Yes, but if your father wakes up, he'll shoot me.'

'But he won't wake up, otherwise I wouldn't ask you.'

Suddenly I found them in front of me; I should have moved aside to make way for them, instead I remained still, blocking their way.

'Do you live here?' I asked.

'Yes, I live here, why?' the girl answered.

'I heard what you were saying. If you want you can make love at my house.'

The boy smiled widely with approval, apparently relieved to have survived the challenge she had set him; she stood still and I feared she would refuse.

'My name is Marco,' I added, standing up. The boy, now conclusively won over, as if there were some kind of guarantee in the name Marco, held out his hand to me.

'I'm Luca.'

'And you are Nina.'

'How did you know?' Luca asked, taken aback.

Nina immediately remembered that Luca had referred to her by name a few moments before and emitted a strange, rather hostile, affirmative moan. It seemed she had convinced Luca to overcome his fear and go in with her. If her father caught them, he'd be furious, and the danger had excited her: her knight could prove himself by challenging the dragon. What did this stranger have to do with any of it?

Instead, all three of us walked towards the apartment I rented. Nina and Luca following a few steps behind me holding hands. Going to spend the night in a stranger's house and without the permission of their folks was certainly breaking the rules, and they spoke in hushed tones so as not to be heard.

'He is not a stranger, his name is Marco! Besides, they would never have allowed it.'

They were excited, it was the first time they would spend the whole night together.

I left my bed to them and made myself comfortable on the sofa. In the morning I made some coffee and brought it to the room.

'Did you sleep well?'

'Yes, it's a beautiful bed,' Luca said sitting up. Nina was lying on her side, half asleep; smelling the coffee, her raised hand started to wander in search of the cup and when she found it she leaned on one elbow and started sipping it, her eyes still closed.

The nipples on her small elegant breasts hardened like two seeds protruding from a fruit, I looked at them and Nina covered herself, spilling the coffee on the sheet. Mirroring her movement almost exactly, I turned my head towards the wall. I felt like an intruder. The day had just begun and I already had a good reason to disapprove of myself.

'I'm going to buy a newspaper, so I'll give you time to get up and out of my way.' There was an anger in the tone of my voice that exceeded my intentions. *Why?* I thought, and I would have liked to explain it to her: *It has all been so natural so far: your words, your kisses, my invitation, the sleepy expression on your face as you clung to the cup of coffee. Why have we suddenly fallen into the realm of the forbidden?'*

But I didn't say anything. I was standing in front of them, suspended between, on the one side, the parental prohibitions they had transgressed the night before, the school they had skipped this morning, and their escape from the duties laid out for adolescents to follow, and on the other side, the illusion of love before them, which opened up a universe of possibilities, and was almost compulsory at their age.

They were really young, so naked and fragile in that bed, ready for the onslaught of the years to come that would rain down on their heads like so many stones. How many pairs of lips, sleepless nights, wrong or superficial loves, how many misunderstandings born from an omitted or excessive gesture or a word, how many outbursts lost between narcissism and other intentions would have ground hopes and disappointments into a single mush?

Today they felt it necessary to enchant each other, but soon they will be satisfied with far less. What could they know about these things at their age? Poor guys, so full of love!

I was trying to say these words to myself, one by one, with

a condescending tone to get away from the couple, when the voice once again disappeared down my throat, as if down a black hole into which all reality was swallowed up, a silence that sucked me away from the pair of them in a violent desire not to be there, a wish to disappear. That was solitude. I knew it well from my night walks, and I didn't know how to open a door to step out of it. I was struggling with a mix of things to say or not say, to defend myself or them, or both, or the whole world, to overcome the silence and rebuild the thread of understanding that had broken when I had stared at the girl's hardened nipples. It was the reason I had changed city, to escape a world that was all too clear. I had hoped that everything would still be possible, but instead everything was just as it was.

Nina looked at me, still and attentive as she too looked for a way out with her eyes. Eventually, I untied the knot between us with an indolent gesture that threw my foolishness behind me: I let my body relax from the tension which had kept the couple in suspense, I ran a hand through my hair and let out a breath in which they felt safe; then I went out the front door.

Luca, who hadn't noticed the reason why Nina had spilt the coffee, looked at her moon-eyed, full of joy: 'He's crazy!'

In my eyes she had seen herself ageless. I had looked at her breasts intrusively and she felt more naked than Luca made her feel. Vulnerable, wounded. Stripped of shyness, or gentle discoveries, but left with a dangerous hardness, a body different from the one her lover knew. Luca was the same age as her, they undressed and came together one step at a time, but I had stared at her as an object and had provoked a sudden, dense and ambiguous reaction, of which she was ashamed: defensiveness and a vaguely guilty desire to be more adult, to know how to deal with grown men and be able to tame their aggression. She stared into Luca's eyes, which looked back at her from the enchanted garden of their age, from the love games she had participated in until a few moments before. She now felt separated from those eyes, she looked at them from afar, as from another planet, and tried to call them back to her. She tried to speak; was it worth trying to explain to him? Her voice broke in her throat too and a strange bleat came out making Luca laugh. Then she looked confused at the damp patch on the ceiling. She imagined that right now, at school, the teacher was calling out 'Nina Contin': she had to get up from her desk, and answer his questions.

Luca got up and, happy as a sparrow around bread crumbs on a windowsill, he started a little dance of kisses and toothpaste, chatting and joking, going backwards and forwards from the bathroom. He even hummed a song. Nina sat on the bed for an indefinite length of time, new thoughts criss-crossed her from all directions, from her feet to her head, to her stomach and away, out the window, to home, to school, out to sea.

'Well? Aren't you getting dressed? Come on Nina, the man might come back and get angry; we can have breakfast in the square, then go to pick up the others from school.'

Nina got up, relieved in finding out that it wasn't difficult; she hugged Luca, her friend who had not noticed the strange mood that had conquered her that morning, and that she would not have tried to explain to him. She put on her trousers and shirt and hugged him again. This second hug was almost the proof that she was still a girl, that hugging Luca was as easy as it had always been. However, she realised she was thinking about these things as she held him tight and, when he reached for her mouth to kiss her, Nina hid her lips on his shoulder because she feared he may notice different emotions there.

'Let's go,' she said firmly. Luca ran down the stairs while she slipped on her shoes; before going out she took a last walk around the house, recording every detail with her eyes; it seemed that, one by one, things themselves were going to settle at the back of her mind. She entered the study where I had slept; on the sofa's cushions, there were still traces of my sleep. Half a page of text stuck in the typewriter and many other papers scattered about my desk. 'Forgive me Marco if I hurt you, I didn't want to. Nina' she added on to that half page. Then she too ran down the stairs, towards Luca, towards that age she had become aware of for the first time, feeling it fleeing.

In front of the newsagent's, I regained full possession of that self I had impersonated so many times when waking up in the morning, anxious to start a new life in which work and commitment would keep me busy and prevent me from going out and walking all night without destination or reason. Without hesitation, I bought a newspaper, went into a café, ordered a cappuccino and took out my cigarettes. These were the habits that had sustained several good periods in my life already, allowing me to become passionate about many things, to flow from one day to the next just as the news of this newspaper flowed from one country to another, across totally different parts of the planet, without becoming too attached to any of them. They constituted the repertoire of gestures and thoughts that I seemed to have temporarily abandoned. I was in Venice for a good reason: I was writing about cinema at the time and had come to the Biennale, where for the first time I had regular, paying work. I had been heading down that road, one step at a time and, all of a sudden, I had become a journalist. It was work, I liked it, but from time to time I wondered: was it a *real* job? And did I *really* like it?

At the last festival, I had seen so many films that would be released over the course of the year ahead, I had dozens of reviews pretty much ready to go for the next months. The apartment that the newspaper had found for me had been reasonably affordable so I'd stayed on. Why? Was it me who was making those choices, or was I trying to conform to some vague instructions about how to live life, given by who knows who.

So that morning, like an actor who learns his lines by rote but only finds the true meaning of each phrase and gesture when discussing them with the director, I observed in the others, without irony or malice, how one is supposed to be in the world. I was ready to pepper every exchange with others with appropriate 'please's and 'thank you's, to be offered easily and whenever the opportunity arose. All that was needed was to not feel too much, not worry about what the newsagent thought about his job, life or me, and to not smile or show any particular kindness; then everything would be fine. He would give me the newspaper, of course, I had to remember to pay, and I would sit like everyone else at the café. 'Thank you...' and a smile.

Everything had gone very well. Indeed, I was now sitting in front of a cappuccino and a newspaper; I was reading it or, in any case, I would have been reading it, with a cigarette ready to be smoked between my fingers. I had left the insomnia of the last few days behind me, and soon I would even be resuming work on the interminable translation. I would have liked the company of another human being to share this small success, but it would have been too complicated to explain what the success of such moments meant to me, so, in short, I was better off this way, alone. Staying in Venice had been a good idea, I kept repeating myself, I would soon be getting things organised, it was what I wanted.

I began reading the newspaper: the number of things that were happening that morning was extraordinary; indeed, on the first page, the headlines were printed very large, although none of the articles that followed could actually sustain the drama promised by that font and tone. *Spain Cannot Fail to be Part of Europe* – an opinion that I fully shared and that had always seemed to me beyond any doubt. In the bottom right some football players, always on the front page, happily hugged each other; a caption suggested that a *Turin defeated at home by the newly promoted Como* would have been in trouble. It seemed a bit out of place to publish this news alongside doubts about whether Spain was actually in Europe. But all said and done, it was a beautiful photograph; those players seemed so happy that I thought: *this editor must be a philanthropist!* Then I saw that no less than twelve pages were devoted to sport. And, of course, there was the crime reporting: unfortunate events being told with lightness, cynicism, almost offensive curiosity, like a meal prepared for some beast. My glancing at Nina's breasts reappeared in my thoughts like a wolf wandering around its prey. Just as the voices of the reporters talking about thefts, murders, and small accidents mixed together, so too in me pity, curiosity and ferocity entwined, and I thought once more that this job – despite the precariousness of the contacts I had with the editorial offices – was rapidly becoming mine. I had hardly started and it seemed to me that I had been doing it for too long. But what else could I do? I felt my life flowing like the newspaper's news, something to run to or escape from, quickly and for no real reason. Was that why I ended up in Venice? Tommaso commissioned me every day and I felt comfortable writing for him, about anything. The literary translation that I agreed to do for a small publisher who may never pay me, looked instead interminable, serving only to make me feel more of a literary writer and to protect me from taking journalism too seriously. I didn't want to be occupied by the more important question of what to do with myself: things happened; they would decide for me. Even in the vagueness of my nocturnal wandering these last few weeks, I still managed to write at least one piece a day for the newspaper. Of course, if I really wanted to have a good career as a journalist, Venice made no sense. Besides the Biennale, there was little to report on that would be of interest to a national newspaper. But I had already been through this thought process many times and had come out with no answers. Now I was here, and Tommaso was consistently giving me space for a grounded, level-headed voice in the paper, delivering me into a profession that was somehow taking shape in my life, taming my repulsion for the vagueness of politics, the exaggeration of sport, or the daily domestic dramas that made up so much of journalism. Jealousies and murderers, traffic or work accidents, the suicides of young lovers. After all, even the two kids I had met the night before constituted life, with conflicting families, social backgrounds, and gender perspectives, even they were subjects that could be useful for an article. And I was already wondering: what will I write my next piece about?

I went home, tidied up my desk. I had to translate at least a quarter of a chapter a day. I sat down at the typewriter and reread the half page I had left there. When I found Nina's two-line note, I pulled the page off the roll annoyed: had the small-breasted silent girl repented? It did not move me, nor did it surprise me, at that age you don't even know that saying. 'I didn't mean to' doesn't make any sense at all. Now I had to retype that half page. '"I didn't mean to". Ridiculous! Who did mean to, then? The newsagent?'

I didn't give it another thought and got to work.

Note

1. Literally 'foundation', referring to a pedestrian bank alongside a canal, and working dock – as most Venetian houses' foundations are part of the canal side.

Lagoon

Roberto Ferrucci

I CAN'T STOP TAKING pictures of the big ships; I'm doing it this afternoon with Teresa, just as I did that day at the end of July in 2013. I was sitting in the usual bar, on the Riva dei Sette Martiri, where you barely even notice the passage of the cruise ships anymore. They are a corollary of the view. And they poison it. It's a disturbing juxtaposition that has by now become part of your landscape, integrated into what your eye expects, like a bad habit. For this reason, in Venice, if you've grown accustomed to the mammoth hustle and bustle of big ships over the years, a small change, in what remains an anomaly, catches your eye. And so, that morning at the end of July, the passing of the Carnival Sunshine so close to the bank inevitably made me jump. A few seconds of amazement later and there I was following that impulse – surely new at the time, but soon to become habitual – of pulling out my smartphone and taking pictures or shooting a video. First hand evidence of an obvious spin of the ship's rear, necessary – I guess – to compensate for veering a bit too close to the bank, swinging the stern closer to the shore than I'd ever seen, with a drift that for some seconds seemed unstoppable, catastrophic, before the whole thing finally corrected itself and turned onto the Giudecca Canal. I am a writer and I don't know anything about maritime routes and manoeuvres, but that didn't seem like a normal manoeuvre to me, despite claims made immediately afterwards by the Harbour Office. But what do I know? What remains is the dramatic visual impact: the inertia of the spin, with the ship listing towards the bank. Was it normal for that to be happening just a few dozen metres away from where I was sitting?

Within hours my pictures and video went viral. The photos were published by the then Venice Green Party councillor and writer, Gianfranco Bettin, to whom I had sent them immediately and who, like me, was alarmed by the manoeuvre. And who, like me, found himself the target of a rather clumsy attempt at media retaliation, launched by that small number of people who make exorbitant profits from the cruise industry. All the newspapers and TV channels talked about it, I was interviewed by TG1, and the whole thing was the fourth most important news item of the day, a ranking that not even a Nobel Laureate in Literature would reach in Italy.

It was disturbing evidence. And yes it was new to both of us: me, testifying as any sensible citizen should; and him, spreading the news on behalf of the City Council, openly declaring that ships shouldn't be allowed in the lagoon, even though the Municipality had no jurisdiction over the cruise companies. For a long time now, in Italy, the citizen who follows common sense, who knows their rights and claims them, who knows their duties and fulfils them, runs a risk. The citizen who questions, with clear and well-grounded evidence, in absolute good faith and awareness, what in the eyes of the rest of the whole world is pure madness, is first mocked, then insulted and, in the end, accused of very serious crimes.

I've been sued for endangering navigation, causing alarm, and simulating a crime, by a committee that supports the passage of big ships across the lagoon and is directly linked to the cruise industry. 'You risk years in jail,' a lawyer friend told me, in all earnestness. They described me as a 'manipulator of perspectives', and hired two young detectives to dig up something on me that might support their theory about my friendship with the Green Party councillor – which, for some, was synonymous with intrigue, or fraud – as well as to confirm 'shady' sightings of me in the bar the day before and after the incident. A quick search on Google would have been enough, there was no need for private detectives. (Just think, dear detectives, that I am right here again, at the Melograno Bar, adding this parenthesis as I'm proofreading my book. I am adding it, because even if six years have gone by, it still bothers me to know that a couple of nobodies, hired by a third nobody, intruded into my life to try to find out God knows what. I can just imagine your silly and morbid questions to the bartenders. I just wanted to tell you about my annoyance and I wanted to do it in a book because, you know, books are long-lived things, they last over time, go beyond seasons, ages, lives… even your lives, dear detectives, yours and the lives of those who hired you). A couple of months later, the captain of the ship, questioned by a magistrate – whom, by the way, never summoned me nor Gianfranco Bettin – admitted he had made a more hazardous manoeuvre than usual, because of a ferry coming in the opposite direction, or so he claimed. The case was dismissed in the summer of 2008.

In short, on this occasion, the smear machine – a tiny smear machine, to tell the truth, a bargain-basement version of it – set in motion immediately after media outlets all over the world picked up the story, didn't work. And neither, unfortunately, did our evidence of a narrow escape, a disturbing anomaly. The ships are still there, despite the demonstrations, despite the petitions, despite the citizens' committees against them. They parade around the lagoon undisturbed and in ever greater numbers, bigger and more polluting. Luckily, my primary school teacher, who taught me citizenship, will never know how useless his efforts were. Or mine.

Then it happened again, years later. I was there, as before, on a Sunday, in the middle of writing a book – on Antonio Tabucchi this time – with the black sky behind San Marco, still and threatening. All the weather apps concurred: 100 per cent likelihood of heavy thunderstorms at around 6pm. And shortly after 6pm, a strong wind announced what was to follow. I moved inside the bar, sat at the farthest table and got back to work, earphones at almost maximum volume, U2, I think, or a seventies playlist. It was then a thundering noise drowned out both my music and the voices around me. I looked up and saw hailstones, big as golf balls, bouncing off the little tables outside. I grabbed my iPhone, headed for the door and began filming the hail. But then something else entered the frame, for three minutes and fifty seconds. The next day, *La Repubblica* asked me to write about it. Which I did.

This second video also went viral. I'm not proud of it, as once again it was about a near-tragedy, involving a cruise ship in Venice. After half of the world had watched it, I was asked: Can you describe to us what you saw? But how can I? How are you supposed to describe certain images? Even if you were a writer who happened to shoot a video like the one I did on Sunday, 7 July 2019 on Riva dei Sette Martiri in Venice, what words would you use to recreate the power of that moment, the sounds, the emotions, the amazement and, above all, the fear? No doubt you would reach for some little used, rare, indisputable phrases, but in the end, the video would still speak for itself. Words would only ever be a caption, an added extra, and in any case they would sound muffled, reassuring even by comparison. Yet we have to try. I have been going to the Melograno Bar in Riva dei Sette Martiri to write since 2002. I have seen hundreds and hundreds of cruise ships passing by. I have also been there on Sundays. Then came the storm, announced by all the weather forecasters and clearly visible, for some time, in the sky behind San Marco. The customers on the terrace took shelter inside. As it grew dark and the surrounding landscape quickly disappeared, obliterated by the storm and the hail, I looked through the doorway to film those gigantic ice-balls that threatened to smash those tables outside to pieces. Across from us, everything had disappeared: the island of San Giorgio, the lagoon, San Marco, everything. Then a puff of smoke entered the frame first – black, much blacker than the dark grey wall created by the storm – the smoke of a tugboat that had been struggling with forces hitherto unseen. Until that moment when suddenly, immediately behind it, and just a few metres beyond the bank, the massive, imposing anvil of the bow of a cruise ship appeared. And from that moment, the storm became 'Deliziosa', delicious. Not even the bravest writer would have dared to be so ironic with the choice of name he gave the Costa Cruises ship.

I continued filming, as the hail became something of an insignificance and the Deliziosa veered first towards the bank in front of me and then the luxury yacht berthed further downstream. When the bow bore down on the yacht and the siren went off – horrifyingly – the passengers of the yacht started jumping overboard, terrified to the point of seeming suicidal. By this point, however, the struggle between the little tugboats and the deranged mammoth was over, a victory for the underdogs, thanks to the captains, and to fate as well. When this video went viral I received requests from all over the world, bringing with it a realisation: it would be the rest of the world, not us Venetians, nor even us Italians, who would save Venice.

Alternatively, we could consider the photo I took one evening in July, a couple of weeks after the aforementioned near-miss at sunset – a purple, lilac, blue, yellow sunset – with a cruise ship leaving Venice, black against the light, with San

Marco in the background. We were on the vaporetto returning from Lido, and there, above the magnificent skyline of the island of San Giorgio with its tree-lined park: two vermilion-coloured flames, tens of metres high accompanied by black smoke, slightly darker than what comes out of the ship's chimney.

Half the city – the one that saw only the smoke and glow of those flames – believed it to be a fire, and as every Venetian does on such occasions, they immediately thought of the evening of 29 January 1996, when the La Fenice Theatre was burned to the ground. This time, however, it was the two torches of the Versalis cracking plant, burning tons of toxic substances: ethylene and propylene. The preposterous municipality website kept posting that everything was fine, that the air quality was still OK, as if the emissions of the big ships were as sweet as eucalyptus and menthol. The flames could be seen from miles away, and every time you did see them, you feared the worst. Assuming it was not, in fact, the actual worst.

In the first half of 2019, there was an accident every month. Compressor blockage in April, plant restart in May, pump failures in June and July. The natural colours of the city that evening – marvellous; the shadows of the palaces, bell towers and churches – splendid, against the richly-hued backdrop of the sunset; but then the whole image made putrid by the ship and the torches firing flames and poisons into the sky. Harmless? And some idiot still insists on having the cruise ships park right there.

Alone or with Teresa, sitting down to write or walking hand in hand, I often raise my eyes just as a ship detaches itself from the dock of the Maritime Station and its imperious bow starts to loom over the city even before it passes through it. The absurd steel iceberg disappears after turning portside, towards the Giudecca Canal. Now the big ship overlaps with the spectacle of Porto Marghera, behind it: smoke on smoke (sometimes smoke on flames); tons on tons. Clearly that landscape in the background, already so incongruous, so out of place, so toxic, was not enough. There was apparently a need to add even more metal, poison, and danger, even if only in transit. Yet, it is a never-ending transit. Permanent now. The number of fine particles released into the air by a single cruise ship is equivalent to fourteen thousand cars running around for one day. A floating eco-monster, advancing towards the San Marco basin where, a little further down, the old man of the lagoon is already reeling in the line of his fishing rod, wheezing.

I would really like the saboteurs of the landscape to listen to him one day, the old man of the lagoon, and ask him about these fumes. Because he knows. They could catch him on his corner as he quickly reels in his line, and he would make a list of all the pollutants present in the dust particles emitted by those monsters. He would do it calmly, precisely articulating the names of the poisons that pollute the air of Venice: Pm10 and Pm2,5, nitrogen dioxide, carbon dioxide, polycyclic aromatic hydrocarbon, benzoapyrene, benzene, as well as heavy metals and dioxins. He would take a pause after this litany recited without taking a breath, then he would say, 'Do you understand, dear sirs? Poisons concentrated together in those little black, fetid clouds that according to you – tell me if I'm wrong, dear saboteurs of the landscape, pillagers of the lagoon – emit sweet wafts like eucalyptus and menthol.' He wouldn't give them time to reply. He would nail them with a look, the old man of the lagoon, he would enjoy their embarrassment, watch them sweat for a moment, or throw in some data from a research study – a tragic one – carried out in Civitavecchia: the population residing within five hundred metres of the harbour where the ships moor can expect a mortality rate increase of 31 per cent in lung cancer cases and

51 per cent in cases of neurological diseases. Not to mention the fish. He would have told them about his fish, by now disappeared from these waters, thanks to the emissions of the big ships, and the millions of tons of steel that have been roving around unpunished for years, devastating the lagoon's fragile seabed. 'And so, now' – the old man of the lagoon might conclude, a little melodramatically, as he looked the cruise company owners straight in the eye – 'now, I am forced to wind in my reel for the final time; and it will creak in the emptiness left by your final devastation.' And if next to him that day stood Teresa's counterpart, the old woman of the who-knows-what, those men dressed in suits and ties would have had to hear her exasperated 'Maria Signor Benedeto!'[1] – Benedeto with one T, as we Venetians always ignore the double letters – and her declining their formalities, shaking only her head, and that would have been enough to make them feel even more uneasy, even more guilty. Maybe.

When the mastodons pass by, the people on the banks always look up in admiration; gigantic things always amaze us. They scare us, but it's a perverse, attractive fear that seduces us. It becomes a simple aesthetic fact. A collective 'ooooohhh', shared by adults and kids alike. On board, up there, perched dozens of metres above the surface of the lagoon, we can make out slight, dark, vaguely anthropomorphic shadows. Figurines made flesh, taken straight from a multilingual brochure that promises cruise-goers a breath-taking view of Venice, from there, from above. And from the water. Dark silhouettes waving their hands – once again – *ciao, ciao* – as well as firing tiny white lightning bolts, flash after flash, another promise of the brochure: pixels to be sent immediately, via mail or WhatsApp, to relatives and friends. Instantly shared on Facebook, Twitter, Instagram. Dark bodies faintly outlining the hundred thousand tons of machinery ploughing through the delicate waters of the lagoon, millions of kilograms disturbing the stones of Venice, shaking the windows of the houses, making floors tremble, foundations stagger, but apparently leaving the water around them perfectly intact. You see − say the conmen of common sense, the pillagers of the lagoon to those raising the issue − these ships don't make waves. Except that, here it is, several minutes later, the suction and piston effect, and you on the pontoon, waiting for a vaporetto, suddenly feeling the floor moving under your feet, as if racked by a storm that isn't there, as if a cruise ship were passing by, as if tons of goods were passing by, which is what actually happened, indeed, but a few minutes ago, not now, and the wave surges from the depths, millions of litres of displaced water, violated a few minutes before, because a body can't plough the sea without displacing an equivalent quantity of it, of the sea that is.

Of the lagoon, in this case, which is not the sea.

The conmen of common sense, the pillagers of the landscape know all this perfectly well: a suction and piston effect, that suddenly empties the canals, only to refill them again, just as suddenly, causing initially almost imperceptible, mini-tsunamis that, in the long run, will prove devastating for canal banks, foundations, and the buildings of Venice generally. Finally, as if this weren't enough, there are the big propellers, hidden down below, that lift and whisk and scatter sediments, that upturn and upset the seabed. Week in, week out, there's a perpetual coming and going in Venice. As if great lorries thundered through Milan's Piazza Duomo, or tanks crossed Florence's Ponte Vecchio, or planes landed on the Champs Élysées in Paris or trains cut Rome's Piazza Navona in two... every day, only multiplied. Because Venice is Venice. So ask yourself what happens to the foundations of Piazza San Marco, when those floating cities, by no means invisible, consisting of millions of kilos of steel, glass, plastic, liquids, humanity... what happens when all that passes, pressing down with all that tonnage, that strength, that unprecedented power, down and down towards the roots of the world's most beautiful, most fragile city, mine.

Having reached their destination, passing parallel to Piazza San Marco, come six o'clock, or half-past six, or seven in the evening, more or less every thirty minutes – noisy and imposing and interfering – the ships start to leave the city, there, in front of Palazzo Ducale, darkening it in the setting sun. At this point, the dark profiles of the passengers, all clustered together up there against the light, finally reach their apotheosis of clicks, jostling to get the best shot. From down here, far below, someone wishes that a smartphone would slip out of somebody's hand, aided by the humidity or the emotion or an unintentional elbow, to go plop, straight down into the water. From down here, that's what we think about to sublimate at least some of the anger. A few seconds after they pass, the people on the bank will be hit by a gust of artificial wind, the reverberation of tons of air, no different to water in this regard. And then the smoke, up there, uninterrupted, black. Even blacker against the light. Poisonous.

Note

1. 'Mary, Blessed Lord', as an exclamation.

Why I Begin at the End

Ginevra Lamberti

I COME FROM THE countryside originally, from a small village at the foot of the mountains. Only an hour and a half by train separates the village from this island that is not an island, but rather an absurdity of engineering standing in a lagoon.

All in all, I have been living in Venice for fourteen years. I moved here to study at the university, and decided to stay because it's always easier to find work in places where large numbers of humans congregate.

This business of moving from the countryside to urban centres in order to find a job is a phenomenon that I've been studying since primary school, which is why, when the time came to put it into practice, it didn't surprise me much. This phenomenon is called urbanisation or *de-ruralisation* depending on whether you look at it from the perspective of the city or from the countryside.

The thing that perhaps experts on human movement commissioned to write school textbooks did not expect is that, in its current state, the urban centre of Venice is actually inhabited less by settled humans, than by wandering ones.

The wandering ones are the tourists, almost 30 million of them walk through this city every year. I would like to feel sad about it, and indeed I do feel a little sad when I indulge my more apocalyptic thoughts, but the fact is that tourists pay for the food on my table, my dentist bills and any shopping sprees I decide to go on, even the occasional wax.

However, I didn't want to talk about this, in as much as this is exactly what I wanted to talk about, but I also wanted to talk about other things, for example the fact that despite the holidays, despite work, despite study, despite life, at some point all of us die.

What I do When I'm Not Writing (Cleaning)

Today I sanitised the tumble dryer because a Polish guy decided it was a good idea to ejaculate on it. I felt a little offended because the tumble dryer is something I think I will always consider as one of the great achievements of the modern world. Then I wondered if perhaps he, like so many of us, had also lived much of his life without the benefit of certain everyday household appliances. Maybe he became overwhelmed. *How can I get angry in the face of such emotion?* I asked the rubber gloves, the spray bleach, the tumble dryer itself, and the vein throbbing on my forehead. Emotions are important.

It was 1 March 2014, still Carnival time, when Giulia and I landed here in this apartment, on the third floor, safe from the acqua alta, barring end-of-the-known-world type catastrophes. It had white walls, two large double bedrooms for single use and a third room to sublet to 'global pilgrims' by application only, thus making us all serfs (vassals? vassals' serfs?) of the sharing economy to cover rent while juggling two or three other, unrelated jobs. Dreaming – without being bold enough to get our hopes up – of one day investing in a city that, two hours after the climate catastrophe strikes, will be engulfed by waves. For the moment, let's try to familiarise ourselves with the algorithm.

In recent times this system has been very popular due in part to the increase in rents / In recent times this very popular system has been increasing rents. I would like to propose one of these two variants, or both, with steadfast certainty, but it must be said that the rents were unreal even back in 2005, when, along with other students, I was crammed into the dilapidated former convent's warehouse, for the first time getting used to the concept of substandard.

As I was saying, this system is now structured so that, while travelling, you can go and stay in people's homes instead of at a hotel, and you can choose whose house to stay at based on reviews you've read by other users. It's the net sum perfectibility of every known system, and I don't think it's that unreasonable, because I have always slept on friends' sofas and floors, sometimes on complete strangers' sofas and floors. The way I see it, it's a form of couchsurfing where you pay a contribution appropriate to your means, and which basically secures a bed and four walls instead of a floor in a corridor. And then there's the added bonus of not being raped and killed.

On the flip side, what you get to do is make the rooms of your house available to guests or travellers or tourists, whom we will refer to as 'global pilgrims' from here on in. You do this hoping it will be a positive experience, and that over the years you will accumulate anecdotes that, you know, might come in handy.

The algorithm, as I mentioned, has plans for your life. It composes risky aggregations following its own unquestionable logic. It works like capitalism, of which it is a child, but isn't as subtle. It stutters if people come to blows because the intersection of data puts a Chinese and a Japanese person together (they're both Asian!), an Israeli and a Tunisian (they both speak Semitic languages!), a Russian girl with two Ukrainians (they both write with the same funny characters!). In this sense, it is never entirely certain, but at least likely, that the algorithm also knows who will be unable to open the door, and who will lose or break the keys. It puts them in your house all at once, perhaps thinking that this relieves you of needing to spare them any thought yourself.

Now let's talk about the fact that nothing is forever, not even living together, not even – unthinkable though it is – living together with friends and roommates.

I didn't know how to explain the new situation without washing too much of our dirty linen in public so I took the liberty of sending a message to Giulia, asking her: *Giulia, in explaining why our residential and professional paths separated, can I write that you were fed up with working with tourists in the house, while I was fed up with working with tourists outside the house? Would you say that this is a fairly comprehensive and, at the same time, discreet summary?* Then I waited for an answer. Soon I would know if the paragraph needed updating.

In the meantime, I'll fast forward a bit. Our residential paths have indeed separated, and my ten-year experience of living with roommates has come to an end, to make way for the professional rentalisation of *two* rooms – rather than one – with a shared bathroom and the endless struggle for a morning pee that comes with it. On top of this, I also had to make room for a newcomer, my partner Sacca, and subsequently the creation of the concept of the super-studio apartment with an open-plan wardrobe.

A super-studio apartment is when you live with your life partner in one room in an apartment shared with other tenants, characterised precisely by a shared bathroom, semi-habitable kitchen, and the absence of any living room, because that bourgeois relic has long since become another bedroom. In the super-studio apartment, equality between individuals is defined by the fact that nobody has a room entirely to themselves.

An open-plan wardrobe is what happens to every surface of your super-studio apartment, including the floor, once you realise that traditional wardrobes and drawers are not enough to contain the belongings of two people.

However, there were moments when we set the bar of possible difficulties even higher than that of three people living together, on average, for a year. Some years it was four or five, if you consider the variable of global pilgrims on rotation. To pay homage to that year, which we will remember also as the year in which Giulia and I more than once pissed in plastic bottles cut in half, I want to recall the moment in which we fought the forces of evil – the forces of evil being some old French people.

At first, we really *did* adore old people, they were among the most welcome pilgrims. We saw them as disciplined and respectful; they would go to sleep early and wake up early, and spend all day out and about because they didn't have time to waste. But we were told that that had just been good luck on our part. They were a generation just like any other, they had their pretensions and tantrums; they were arrogant. But we continued, open and trusting with others, with everyone, even with the Swedish lady who kept salami in her room so she could have it for breakfast.

Then one day a reservation was made by a guest in his seventies, François, which we gladly accepted. *Come, François, we are waiting for you!*

However, on the day of the check-in instead of François, an old woman arrived in a candy pink dress, like a First Communion dress. She didn't speak a word of anything other than French.

François had sent us a text, which feels like the equivalent of sending a carrier pigeon, saying that she was his sister and that he had booked it on her behalf, as she couldn't do it. He said that he would stay somewhere else and would occasionally bring her home in the evening. Now, I wouldn't like to share too many details of our coexistence with that lady for the following four nights, but I want to, at least, list some key elements, underscoring them with the use of the phrase *your granny in a candy pink dress*.

Therefore, dear reader, try to imagine your grandmother in a candy pink dress, coming back at three in the morning, wandering round the house until 5 o'clock turning the lights on and off, opening and closing all the drawers in the common areas, oven included.

Imagine your granny in a candy pink dress, after spending the night at the casino, locking herself in the bathroom to throw up and then refusing to clean it up because she is tired and a bit, you know, old.

Imagine your granny in a candy pink dress coming home with a certain François, her so-called brother, who for some reason avoids showing his face at all costs. For example, if you go to the kitchen, pretending to be thirsty, you will see François looking out the window into the darkness, with his hands behind his back, and while you speak to him he will never once turn round. Or François sitting on a chair, with his elbows on his knees, staring at the ground, muttering that he is just about to leave. Imagine your granny in a candy pink dress, who, on the last night, at two in the morning, enters the darkness of your own room, slamming the door against the doorframe, and then runs away cursing, and promptly transforming once more into the helpless old woman who says *sorry sorry* but can't answer basic questions such as what she was doing in your room, because she doesn't understand a damn thing, or pretends not to.

At some point, in the past few months, I wanted to insert into this part of the story a scene where I was watching the spectacle of Cristiano Ronaldo surrounded by moths in the middle of the field at the Euro 2016 final. Treacherously brought down by the French, he sits in tears on the ground, with a moth on his nose, soaked, with hundreds of other moths swarming around him. We don't know where they came from, but it is clear that they came for him. Blinded with rage at the thought of Cristiano crying, I imagine smashing the old woman's head with the most classic of ashtrays, and then all three of us – Giulia, Sacca and I – disposing of the corpse. After all, the canal is just below the house, it's child's play to make a corpse disappear here. Her death will never be avenged as no one will ever try to account for it, François will disappear forever revealing the fact that he never really existed.

Luckily for the old woman, I never get round to actually writing any stories, and she was able to return home unscathed both in reality and fiction. Although not without first stealing all the little cents from the tip jar, both in reality and in fiction.

Meanwhile, Giulia has now replied to my message, saying: *Of course, I was fed up with having tourists in our house! It got to the point where I was opening the doors to vagabond-types; it was a form of self-harm the nature of which has yet to be fully defined.*

What I do When I'm Not Writing (Acquire a Place, at Least in this Life)

The Mortgage

Aside from cleaning houses, picking up people to give them the keys, explaining how not to blow the power, and going back in the middle of the night because they *have* blown the power, I have recently found this other occupation called ghost mortgaging. The ghost mortgage works roughly the same as your more familiar ghost shopping.

I am sure everyone knows about ghost shopping, but I will give a practical example all the same, namely that day I went for a walk around the shops with Giulia, Silvia and Norman. We were browsing the spring-summer garments of a large clothing chain for forty-year-olds wanting to dress like fifteen-year-olds, when Norman, pointing to a pinafore decorated with flowers and pheasants, exclaimed, not without a certain satisfaction, 'This shop is full of early Christianity!' Without buying anything, we were quickly shown the door after having thrown shade at every single item.

I believe that my passion for the ghost mortgage was triggered by a painting by a friend of mine, as well as by the fact that, there are more and more people roaming around everywhere in uncontrolled ways. Gertrude Stein said something similar in 1937, and I'm convinced that if Gertrude Stein could take a tour of Venice's streets today she would immediately kill herself. In truth, there are more and more people in the streets so if I spend more time indoors at least I see fewer people at a time. However, I can't always stay inside the super-studio apartment because then I would go crazy, and I can't even sneak illegally into someone else's house. So, I thought, a ghost mortgage would be the most balanced solution.

The best things about ghost mortgages are the landlords. The most interesting ones are the hardest to reach, and it's not just me who thinks this. My friend, for example – the one with the painting – once rang all the bells in his building to find out if anyone knew the owner of the vacant apartment on the ground floor. It was a large place, as you could gather from the outside, with a double entrance and a whole system of long, narrow courtyards surrounding the perimeter, visible from the communal courtyard. In short, the apartment was huge, with something like five rooms and two bathrooms as well as a kitchen. Or so we calculated. And so it was confirmed when, after harassing every private tenant, law firm and B&B in the building, my friend finally managed to make direct contact with the landlord. He was an old lawyer, still in business, who sent his wife to open the place up. I went to see the property too, and that was the moment where we pretended to be a couple of artists in search of large spaces that could be both a home and a studio. We did it out of boredom and for love of the pantomime. At least as far as I was concerned. My friend was actually looking for a property to buy and must have thought the idea of the young couple would play in his favour. I wanted to tell him that the only thing that works in your favour in these cases is being from three generations of wealth, but I suspected deep down he already knew that, so I said nothing.

The wife, as it turned out later, was younger than the old lawyer, but since the latter was actually a *very* old lawyer then his wife was also... let's say mature and came with various tics that had built up over decades of using psychotropic drugs.

The apartment inside was exactly as my friend had imagined it, and besides it was clean, bright and dry despite being on the ground floor, and empty for almost a decade. Now you might say *So what*, but it must be understood that, living every day immersed in a seaweed soup, you eventually learn that trying to slow the process of decomposition is a daily struggle that you must undertake not only with your body but with walls and all other material possessions, as decay is always just around the corner.

After the landlord's wife came the landlord. In fact,

following a strained telephone courtship, the day arrived when we stood at the foot of his office building and then climbed the stairs. Suddenly everything seemed older, as that advert once said, resembling a philosophical thought but in reality just selling a big car; 'Suddenly everything looks brown,' I said. Inside it was all wood: the floors were wood; the walls were panelled with wood; the ceilings were wood and very low as well. That is, high enough to stand upright but low enough to give you the impression it would be better to bow your head a little. Judging from the furnishings, a badly seeded gravitational wave seemed to have thrown us into a detective story set in 1972. The secretary, seeing us, replaced the handset of the round-dial telephone (for the benefit of younger generations, I recommend you google this because it is difficult to explain) and from behind the bulletproof glass of her office, she signalled us to wait a moment as she went to call the boss. Beyond all reasonable expectations, the boss was not an inspector ready to furnish us with the details of a heinous murder, but a lawyer, and the owner of the aforementioned property. I was wearing a worn sweater, but at least not moth-eaten. I put on a stupid smile, while my friend explained that he had serious intentions with respect to the purchase of his empty property due to his imaginary plans relating to family-building, scaling up space-wise, putting down roots.

Keeping his back straight, he lowered his voice a notch and asked for information on the state of the facilities and the price per square metre. Pretending to give us credence, although not too much, the landlord sighed and began answering. On the sheet of paper in front of him, he drew pointless lines and non-existent patterns. His jacket was not worn, but a dark blue that went with all the wood around him, just as the white of his shirt matched the white of his hair. He had broad shoulders despite his age and seemed tall even when seated, or perhaps it just seemed that way because of all the low-hanging wood. Perhaps it was all calculated to make him look taller and his interlocutors look smaller. He said, 'I know this has nothing to do with anything, but I am eighty-two years old and my wife and I have no children; the prices are currently between four and five hundred per square metre, but as a favour to you, I can offer you six hundred thousand for the whole place, but we can't really go below that. But, you know, that's not the point. The point is that, right now, I wouldn't even know where to put six hundred thousand euros, and to be honest, in fifteen years or so, I have no intention of leaving such a sum to any heirs.'

The Painting

Now, I want to explain better the role of this friend of mine in the development of the ghost mortgage technique. There was a time when we worked together in a restaurant, but we weren't really friends as such, partly because he had a habit of not talking to strangers, even though he saw the same ones every day, for years, which actually made them not really strangers anymore. This was something I always respected, so I decided immediately that he would be my imaginary friend, and, in fact, things were going great between us. Then one day, some time after I'd quit that job, we crossed paths again and accidentally started talking to each other. It thus transpired that, on the one hand, I had a book coming out and, on the other, I had already started renting rooms to global pilgrims in order to avoid bankruptcy. In return, it transpired that he painted and found this idea of global pilgrims interesting and potentially useful to him. In the end he was working two jobs and a total of 60 to 70 hours a week, I think, plus overtime, and every now and then when he was about to go nuts, he just went onto the balcony and threw paint on a canvas. Given that he does not have the gift of ubiquity, I now do the cleaning and arrivals when needed, so in conclusion we can say that we are colleagues again and that I was right to think we were friends even before we actually spoke.

Before proceeding with the main point of this section – i.e. a painting, or rather, *the* painting – I want to say that this could be interpreted as a narrative of frustration which perfectly captures the discomfort of today's thirtysomethings, but the truth is cleaning houses is, all in all, something I quite like doing. Specifically, I like dealing with inanimate objects, which I consider myself as having limited responsibilities towards. Sometimes I also like going to collect people, which, of course, contradicts my point about inanimate objects, but I have to say something else I like doing is mixing things up a bit.

Anyway… I was saying that my friend paints. Mostly abstract stuff with materials stuck on it in high relief. That doesn't sound nice, but his works have a charm of their own. For example, the other day I was at his place to arrange the cleaning shifts for the month ahead and we started staring at his latest work. Eventually, I found the courage to break the silence and ask him what the hell it was. He paused dramatically and said: 'This latest piece is called *The Mortgage*. The blue in the upper half represents life in its most authentic state and the circular shape in the top left is "The Being". In the lower half, we see a black parallelepiped emerging from the canvas; that is "The House". It stands out against a black background because everything that is touched by the mortgage deteriorates. The cannulas that come out of the parallelepiped to sink into the circular shape clearly represent the progressive consumption of The Being, inexorably emptied of all beauty by the mortgage.'

We looked at it a little longer, in silence.

What I do When I'm Not Writing
(Go to the Cemetery)

Art. 3 – The Scattering of the Ashes
2. The scattering of ashes must take place during the day through funeral homes or through one's own means, provided that public dignity is guaranteed, in compliance with the regulations in force in the area being scattered and is allowed in the following places in the territory of the Municipality of Venice:

a) in the area intended for this purpose located within the municipal cemeteries of Mestre Centro, Marghera and San Michele in Isola, called "Memory Gardens";
b) in private areas, outdoors, outside built-up areas, with the consent of the owners;
c) outdoors, in the following places:
Mestre Wood;
– The Adriatic Sea, at least 700 metres from the shore;
– North Lagoon: in the area behind the San Michele Cemetery on the south side.

Art. 4 – The Communitarian Sense of Death
In the following cases, so that the communitarian sense of death is not lost, a searchable registration method is set up within the cemeteries, showing the personal data of the deceased whose ashes have been scattered: [...]

Municipal Regulations, Venice

'In 1999,' Sacca says, 'I graduated in science and then enrolled in industrial chemistry, so the year when I changed faculty and enrolled in architecture was the one after that. It must have been in my second year, more or less around this time (namely Tuesday 13 November), because this is when the cemetery hours change. It was Autumn 2001. I had to prepare for an exam on Semerani, who was famous for a project, which, as far as I know, never materialised, for the great cemetery of Pesaro. It was a peculiar design – I can't say I know Pesaro as I've never been there – but it is on the sea and I understand there's a hill behind the city. Semerani's idea was to extend the cemetery up the side of the hill, with a particular emphasis on lighting. The citizens of Pesaro would then be able, at least in theory, to recognise from the city centre, let's say from the town squares, the particular candle of their loved one. Hang on, I think I just heard a noise coming from over there – that family chapel thing.'

'It was my stomach, I think.'

'I get you, all this smell of death has triggered a certain appetite in me too. Let's have fried chicken after. Anyway, the exam consisted of developing a plan for a cemetery. The most ambitious students tried their hands at an expansion project for a pre-existing cemetery, even though, from the academic point of view, it was easier to design one from scratch. I was actually drawn to the cemetery of Palmanova, a very particular city because of its nine-pointed star layout. As a city, it had successfully defended itself against everyone except Napoleon because it always had the most advanced guns. The Palmanova cemetery took up something of this fortification concept, and I liked to fantasise about its expansion. For inspiration, I visited the finest examples of cemetery expansion, such as the Chipperfield project, the more modern part of San Michele Cemetery.'

You know what, I have to stop you there, Sacca.

I had to stop him there because I need to quickly explain that the cemetery of San Michele is the city's cemetery, and if it is true that Venice is an island located in a lagoon, then it is also true that the cemetery of San Michele is itself a smaller island a short vaporetto ride away from the main island, just one stop after the hospital of Santi Giovanni e Paolo. It is a beautiful cemetery, I come here at least once a year to take a tour and to pay respect to someone who is in the new, although not the brand new, section. He is called Constant Fear and is buried right under Severed Mary. Anyway, like all cemeteries, San Michele is divided into sections; the most visited, partly because the celebrities hosted there, are the orthodox, catholic and evangelical sections. There you can find Joseph Brodsky, Igor and Vera Stravinsky, Sergei Diaghilev, Ezra and Dorothy Pound, and Helenio Herrera. Of course, I didn't know who Helenio Herrera was, but as the two of us were wandering round the evangelical section, Sacca smiled a big, 32-teeth smile and said 'Helenio, what are you doing here?', while pointing to a plaque decorated with an Inter Milan scarf.

Now you can go on.

'The Chipperfield project was highly and internationally criticised, and the result of a competition between architects from all over the world. It involved expansion onto an already emerged but unused part of the island, as well as the addition of a piece of artificial island. But the loudspeaker said the cemetery closes at 6.30pm – in other words, soon.'

'Yes, and since you were about to veer off into the Napoleonic foundation of the cemetery, perhaps we could skip a few steps and jump to the point when you first arrived here, in 2001, in order to avoid repeating the same mistakes you did back then, now.'

'At the time there wasn't that loudspeaker, or maybe there was and I ignored it, but I don't think so. Anyway, on that occasion I discovered, at my own cost, that a peculiarity of the San Michele cemetery is that it has different hours to the mainland cemeteries. Wait, there, another noise! Did something move?'

'What? No, don't worry, it was just someone who works here, behind the chapel.'

'Was it?'

'Yeah.'

'No, by this point they would be packing up and getting ready to leave.'

'I don't think so... anyway, you were saying?'

'Well, in short, everything was very quiet and peaceful, but then it began to get dark and I was in a section – I don't remember which – looking at the graves when I found myself standing next to a very old man. This gentleman greeted me – I don't remember the conversation – I assume he started it, as I was entirely occupied with my own business. At one point he asked me what I was going to do, since the cemetery was now closed and there was no keeper. I was stunned because only then did I realise I had been wandering around in a closed and deserted place for more than an hour. This gentleman was a missionary friar, he was dressed in a white tunic, which now I say it doesn't sound very credible, I realise that.'

'Did he have a beard?'

'He had a long white beard.'

'Sure.'

'In any case, he told me he lived there. I don't remember how the conversation developed, because right then, to be honest, I had little interest in knowing where he lived – I was trapped in that place and it was starting to get dark and cold. Then the customary respect you pay very old people led me to accept the direction of the conversation, and in any case he didn't answer the few questions I asked. Instead, he carried on telling me about his missions in Africa. Only after another good hour did he reveal that if I went back to the entrance of the cemetery, and turned to the access door, on the right, about twenty metres away, I would see a small closed door with a latch and a padlock, and that the padlock was only hanging there unclosed, and all I had to do was lift it out of the latch to open the door and thus exit onto the pier. From there he advised me to reach out and wave to draw the attention of some passing vaporetto that would swing by and take me on board. He claimed he was 98, something like that. What do you say, shall we go now? It's almost half past four, we should check where the door to the pier is, which obviously we won't be able to find.'

And, in fact, we didn't find it, finding instead a door that opened onto the churchyard of the Calmaldolese Monastery closed since 1910, a churchyard overlooking the lagoon, overlooking the water, without a pier.

25th April 2020

Annalisa Bruni

THE TABLE ON THE altana is set: a jug of Campari spritz, a bottle of prosecco, some freshly baked pizza snacks, pretzels, a plate of cold cuts, a diced onion omelette, mixed vegetables au gratin, a bowl full of cherry tomatoes and some tzatziki sauce with crostinis on the side.

LUCIA: 'What do you think, will this do the job?'

PAOLO: 'Well, this is an aperitif, right, not a reception? You do have a habit of cooking for an army. That said, under the current circumstances…'

LUCIA: 'The thing is, I thought that – given the time of the meeting – it would end up being our lunch on the 25th April more than a drinks party. You'll see, there won't be any leftovers, as usual. Actually, could you do me a favour and pop down to the kitchen and get the cold pasta, before the others arrive.'

PAOLO: 'You're unbelievable! We can't have them waiting, can we, eh? While I'm downstairs, I may as well get the laptop too, as it's almost time for the meeting.'

LUCIA: 'We agreed 12:30, right?!'

PAOLO: 'Yes, I sent all the invites.'

LUCIA: 'This was a great idea of yours. It will be nice for everyone to be together today. I'm warning you, though, at

3:30pm we're all going to sing "Bella Ciao", and I'm streaming it on Facebook. I won't have any fuss about it. If you don't want to sing, don't!'

PAOLO: 'Thank goodness, there's still a bit of democracy in this house.' Laughing, he heads down the small staircase, immediately after kissing the woman he has been arguing with for thirty-odd years.

ELSA: 'Hi guys. How are you? Is everything fine?!'

PAOLO: 'We're hanging on, Elsa; welcome! As always, the first to arrive is the one who lives furthest away!'

ELSA: 'You should know by now, I'm always on time, if not early; I've been waiting for you to give me access, you know? And what about Lucia, is she here?'

PAOLO: 'She's just gone to get a vase of flowers for the table. She's the same old perfectionist…'

ELSA: 'Which direction? Would you pan around for me? You have no idea of how much I miss Venice!'

Paolo grabs his laptop and turns it around, all along the perimeter of the altana, as if it were a drone doing a shoot for Google Maps. From the small Madrilenian apartment where Elsa is currently stuck, she can hear the shriek of seagulls, and imagines flying over the rooftops until she can see the Giudecca Canal passing through deserted streets and squares and brushing against bell towers lit by a spring sun that makes the water of the canals – extraordinarily clear and still – sparkle.

ELSA: 'Amazing, thank you! It's crazy to see our city so empty and silent. I watched some reports on TV, but it's different to see it for real, from your house.'

PAOLO: 'It's unbelievable for us too. Just going outside – the few times I've been to the office, carrying all my documents, of course, in case the police stop me – and walking alone down the street without meeting a living soul, crossing entire districts without a single shop, bar or restaurant open. It's like living in a ghost town from one day to the next. Incredible to see the lagoon's wide stretch of water so flat and still, without boats, gondolas or vaporettos passing by, to breathe crystal-clear air, to look up and enjoy such an uncommonly clear sky. Even the humidity seems to have gone, you know? These are wonderful days, it hasn't rained for months, like a cruel joke, as we have to stay indoors…'

LUCIA: 'It's ironic, isn't it?' Her face pops out the side of the screen, half-obscured by a bunch of red tulips, among which stands a rosebud of the same colour.

LUCIA: 'We longed so much to have a Venice all to ourselves, and now it's here it feels so disturbing, empty and lifeless. Before it was taken away from us, we felt like guests here, even unwanted ones, and now we can't take pleasure in the situation. We've gone from one extreme to the other, from an overcrowded, unlivable city to this desolation, as if we were living in *The Day After*, or some science fiction film about the end of the world.'

ELSA: 'And yet, despite everything, you managed to have a bocolo,[1] even this year, huh? And you complain about your husband…'

LUCIA: 'Some traditions need to be respected, you know, even if the sky falls in. And what about you and living with Roberto? What's it like for him, having mum in the way all the time, unexpectedly, for god knows how long?'

ELSA: 'It could be worse, I guess. I try not to be a heavy presence. I'm taking the opportunity to read in Spanish, and improve my grasp of it by watching a lot of TV. Making the most of the situation, you know. I hope I'll be allowed back soon, but no one knows anything yet, all flights are suspended.'

PAOLO: 'Show us what nice meal you've cooked, while I let the others in.' He puts the laptop down on the table once again.

One by one, on the screen – next to a wide-shot of cicchetti,[2] that Elsa displays with pride, sardèè in saor,[3] soft-boiled eggs with anchovies, crostinis smeared with tuna mousse together with a pitcher of sangria, to give everything a Spanish touch, as if the dish heaving with jamón serrano wasn't enough – beside this display, the other guests materialise, letting themselves be heard in a growing clamour of happy greetings, kisses thrown in the air, and laughter.

One by one, many frames appear, with views overlooking a balcony (Angela, from her apartment in the centre of Mestre), a garden (Vera and Alessandro, a farmhouse in Trivignano), a living room crowded with bookcases (Sandra and Mario, from their townhouse in Castello), a wide shady terrace (Olga, in Rio Terà San Leonardo in Cannaregio).

Angela has managed to place a small camping table in amongst the flower pots that throng the limited space available and raises her glass of Traminer revealing mozzarella and tomato skewers as well as tortillas next to a bowl overflowing with guacamole.

ANGELA: 'I couldn't put anything else out: I wouldn't have known where to put the tablet. And, you know, it's such a lovely day, I just wanted to be outside. Also I'm on my own, so this is more than enough. It's so nice to see you guys! It's really touching, you know!'

SANDRA: 'Same here. We'll probably start getting emotional if we're not careful.' Sandra's husband sits down on the couch right next to her and proposes a toast to the whole group.

MARIO: 'Cheers! To our continued good health!... is probably the right thing to say, don't you think? Now more than ever, friends. Health, health, health! You all look in good shape, all of you. And it's great!' And he bites into a slice of asparagus quiche.

Different threads of small talk weave together, as do more serious conversations, anecdotes, concerns and hopes.

Each one of the friends has a lot to say, each one is living through an extraordinary experience, inconceivable only a few weeks before, each in a different way.

Those who can count on open space and countryside nearby – like Vera and Alessandro – where they can take stretch their legs safely despite the restrictions realise how lucky they are; those who are retired – like Elsa – think about those who have to continue to go to work each day via overcrowded, cut-back public transport; those who have a regular salary – like Lucia, Sandra and Mario – feel privileged compared to those who've had to close their businesses and might not be able to open them again, when all of this is over (whenever that is).

ELSA: 'You know, guys, on the balcony in front of us, the neighbours hung out a banner that said, *La romantización de la cuarantena es privilegio de clase!*[4] And that's exactly what it is. Only those who can afford it are experiencing this emergency as merely a time to devote to their family, kids, reading, or maybe to enjoy a bit of baking or bricolage. Let's spare a thought for those who live with two, three, or more toddlers, or even worse, teenagers, in 50 square-metre apartments in the middle of cities, and those who have to work from home on top of that.'

ALESSANDRO: 'Indeed, and those who only have one computer between the whole family, or those with bad internet connections that makes everything even harder. You already know – the internet in certain areas of Venice is very up and down.'

OLGA: 'Not to mention domestic violence. I get chills when I think that this pandemic could have happened while I was still married. Can you imagine?'

ANGELA: 'I was right then, never wanting to move in with anyone, let alone wanting to get married!' And she raises her glass, full to the brim with Traminer, as if saying cheers to her own lifestyle.

MARIO: 'Thank you, in that case, on behalf of all the men of the group! Anyway, Olga, you know we would have come to the rescue, honey. We would have never left you alone with him.'

LUCIA: 'I also wonder how we would have reacted if this had happened to us as teenagers. Would we have even been able to bear not seeing a girlfriend, a boyfriend, or not being able to meet with friends? I think about those parents right now that have to deal with the isolation of their kids, locked up in a cage at an age when the tension – or to be kinder, the spirit of rebellion – runs high even on a normal day.' And she bites into a pizza snack.

VERA: 'Well, I for one, would have run away from home by now, at least for a few hours; I know I would.'

SANDRA: 'Yep, you're hot-blooded for sure but also quite the hypochondriac. Are you sure you wouldn't have been too terrified by the thought of the virus? I remember how you freaked out about HIV.'

VERA: 'OK, fine, but I had my reasons back then. Anyway, I've cooled down since those days, haven't I, Alessandro? You've arrived just in time,' and she grabs her husband's chin to kiss him audibly on the lips.

Glasses are drained then filled up again, the same happens with the plates; the conversation heats up and the voices often overwhelm one another in the struggle to talk on a video-link that often freezes or collapses completely. Words or entire sentences get lost, but at least they can be together again and share this difficult moment, so hard for everyone, even if less hard for them than for others. They are well aware of it.

LUCIA: 'What about supermarkets, are you shopping there?'

ANGELA: 'Well, no. Since lockdown, I get my groceries from the small local stores around here, even if they're more expensive. Who cares. In fact, I'm saving some money. What shall I spend it on, anyway? No cinemas, no theatres, no concerts, no restaurants, no coffees, no going for a drink.'

LUCIA: 'My biavarol[5] has a clearly-marked basket for "spesa sospesa"[6] and every time I go there I leave something. Then, in the evening, the shopkeeper takes it all to Caritas. I give what my meagre state salary allows me to.'

MARIO: 'I've heard there's going to be a big, live-streamed event soon with artists, actors, comedians and singers to raise money for workers in the cultural sector, who are one of the less protected groups of workers, nowadays. I'll transfer them some money, I know many people who've had their entire programmes cancelled; none of them knows when they'll be able to get back to work.'

OLGA: 'Sounds good! Send me a link. I'll do the same.'

ROBERTO: 'Hey, can I say hello to the old codgers?'

A chorus of greetings and warm, playful protests greet Elsa's son, who grins at the webcam while pouring himself a large sangria and filling his dish with finger food.

MARIO: 'You won't be young forever, cheeky brat! But we forgive you seeing as you must be finding it so hard being stuck with your mother'.

ROBERTO: 'What about *your* kids? Did you kill them all?'

SANDRA: 'Viola stayed in Milan, she couldn't leave on time, and she graduated all alone in front of her computer.'

MARIO: 'After all these years and so many sacrifices, we didn't even have the pleasure of attending the ceremony. Filippo is here with us, grumbling and bugging us, on the rare occasions he's not studying in his room. This year he has to earn his high-school diploma and we still don't know how he will manage it… But at least he can be home-schooled and that's a relief.'

VERA: 'Ludovica and Martina are at home with their partners, we hardly ever see and hear from them, so no change there then. What matters is that they're fine. As for their "jobs", let's not go there…'

ALESSANDRA: 'Yeah, we try not to stick our nose into our kids' business either.'

ROBERTO: 'Fair play to you. That's the way to do it. Not like a certain person I could mention, who came here for a weekend and never left.'

ELSA: 'He's such a comedian this one! He knows if I could, I'd leave tomorrow.'

ROBERTO: 'Only joking, Mum! Right, best get back to studying. Laters, everyone!', and he disappears, right after filling his glass and dish once more.

ANGELA: 'Luckily, I never…'

A chorus of voices saying 'Yes, sure, we know it, Angela: Luckily you never had kids!' rings out.

ANGELA: 'You might be my lifelong friends, you might know me like the back of your hand, but you are really bloody annoying', and she laughs, pouring some more wine in her – once again empty – glass.

ELSA: 'And what about you, Paolo, how are you getting on with all these decrees to stave off total economic collapse?'

PAOLO: 'Don't even talk about it. I feel like I'm in the trenches, with panicking clients ringing me at every hour of the day. They want to get advice on how to run their business, whether to apply for the special redundancy fund, how to fire workers, but when I don't get any clarity from the government, what can I say? Anyway, let's change the subject, at least for today…'

ELSA: 'You're right. Sorry. Everything seems so strange, from abroad.'

PAOLA: 'And it is. Anyway, give me a quick tour of

Madrid. Come on, go out on the balcony and give us a pan of your street.'

Everyone's screen fills up with a periwinkle sky above a wide boulevard with majestic buildings burned by a blinding sun. The boulevard is empty; no sign of the usual traffic and people so typical of pre-Covid Madrid at most hours of the day.

ELSA: 'You know, every day at 6pm, we go to the window to clap for the frontline health workers.'

LUCIA: 'In Italy, we've been singing from windows and balconies instead. At first, there was a lot of optimism and a sense of desire to rebuild communities. Now it seems to be softening, and being replaced by people reporting on each other. You know, some people call the police if they see someone out for a run or walking their dog, or couples walking hand in hand? And for some weeks there was a blizzard of fines, hundreds of euros at a time. It's like mass hysteria.'

LUCIA: 'Hey, Paolo… where's Riccardo? You invited him, didn't you? It looks like he's the only one who didn't show up.'

PAOLO: 'Shit, you're right! The usual latecomer. It's probably not very PC of me to say it, but in the end, he's still a man from the South, even if he has been living here for thirty years. I'm sending him a text now, let's see if he wakes up.'

RICCARDO: 'I'm here, I'm here! We said 1pm, didn't we?'

The virtual entrance triggers a chorus of affectionate protests, that resound around the small lawn in front of Riccardo's house at Città Giardino in Marghera. The spot he has chosen is laid out with frozen cans of beer, a bag of chips and other junk food.

RICCARDO: 'Please, don't say anything. I know you disapprove, but I'm dismantling the house ahead of the move, so basically I don't cook anymore and you know how much cooking means to me.'

ANGELA: 'So you made up your mind, finally. You're moving back to Sicily for good?'

RICCARDO: 'Absolutely. I've already handed the apartment over to an estate agent and I'm just focusing on the move. I'm trying to sell it furnished, though, as that would be easier. And also more painful, obviously, given my style.'

ANGELA: 'You're always so dramatic, Ricky. Are you retired now?'

RICCARDO: 'Yes, I retired a month ago. I couldn't even celebrate it in the office; we were already working from home. This is why I'm running around. I want to leave as soon as they "unlock the cages". I'm going back to my roots. I've got nothing here – no job, no family, not even a partner? My ninety-year-old mum is all alone over there. I have no more excuses. I'll also finally get to breathe some fresh air, for a change, instead of the noxious vapours of Porto Marghera.'

ANGELA: 'You're right, we manage to block out the thought of it, otherwise we would go crazy, but we all know deep down an environmental disaster could strike at any moment, before the decontamination of that area ever gets completed.'

RICCARDO: 'Indeed, and I just don't want to be around when the next accident happens. And it will happen, you'll see.'[7]

MARIO: 'Come on guys, let's drown our sorrows. As you're all here, we have a good reason to cheer again.'

RICCARDO refills his glass of beer and makes it click against the bottle with a quite theatrical gesture, and says: 'So, except for Paolo – who, since becoming self-employed, won't ever stop working, which makes him happy, I guess – who else is still working among us?'

LUCIA: 'Well, the younger ones, obviously. If I'm lucky, I'll retire in seven years.'

OLGA: 'Tell us, Teach! How's the whole distance learning going? I hear about it all the time, but I can't imagine how you are coping.'

LUCIA: 'Well, precisely: we're 'coping'. If we waited for the minister to explain what we're supposed to be doing... we'd still be waiting! I spend hours and hours everyday video-conferencing with the kids. We teach, correct homework, invite writers and experts to come and liven up the schooling process with new ideas – we've had to make it up as we go along. Can you imagine, I have some students from Bangladesh who were visiting family when this happened and couldn't come back to Italy: they manage to attend lessons via their mobiles, it's admirable. Others have had access issues; I've been able to get some second-hand computers so that they wouldn't be left behind. By the way, thanks everyone who helped with that. But sure, it's sad to see them so far away, and, above all, isolated from their classmates.'

PAOLO: 'And no special thank you for me, for reformatting them all? Typical.'

LUCIA: 'OK, Paolo, we get it! A big thank you to you too, of course! When this pandemic is over, can I send him to you guys for a while? I can't stand him anymore!' She hugs him, as she's saying this, so tight he almost chokes.

VERA: 'And what about you, Sandra? What are you doing while that the museum's closed?'

SANDRA: 'I know you won't believe me, but I'm working harder than ever before and I'm having fun too, but don't tell anyone. It's ironic, isn't it? I spend all day video-conferencing; my colleagues and I invent riddles, comic strips, or games to engage with our social media audiences, exercises and themed activities for children; we plan virtual tours with photos from the archives that we upload onto the museum's website. And let me tell you, we're getting fantastic feedback from the public. We're so thrilled about it. Maybe this is the right time for our director to admit the importance of these channels that he always underestimated or, to be more precise, that he was always a bit sniffy about.'

MARIO: 'I'm working a lot too, you know! The provincial government needed someone to handle the emergency we had with the Ateco codes.[8] I could've kept my head down, but rather than stay all day indoors with Sandra, I volunteered. Basically, everyone who wants to keep working there now has to pass through my clutches, I'm the one issuing permits.'

SANDRA: 'He goes out at seven every morning and comes back at seven in the evening! Guys, it's such a relief for me too! Can you imagine having him around 24 hours a day? I'm not used to it.'

OLGA: 'Mario and Paolo, you're involved in this, in different ways, how is the city doing from your perspectives? Bars, restaurants, hotels all closed…?'

PAOLO: 'Well, how do you think it's doing? It's bad, really, really bad. The tourist industry is in deep shit.'

MARIO: 'Very deep shit. Add to your list taxi drivers, guides, museum workers, travel agencies… I'm surely forgetting someone.'

SANDRA: 'You're forgetting the film industry. Girls, did you know Tom Cruise was here in Venice shooting *Mission Impossible 7*? They had to stop too. One more sector being put through the mill. Besides the actors, there are the technicians, stagehands, makeup artists, costume departments, and so on.'

RICCARDO: 'Well, I've always said Venice can't go on with its touristic monoculture, it needed to reinvent itself, find new economic models. Now we're all desperate for this change, given the conclusive evidence that betting everything on tourism doesn't work. If tourism stops, everything stops. Cruise ships are no longer arriving? It's a tragedy. Planes aren't flying? It's a disaster.'

OLGA: 'Yes, I agree. We need a political class that can look into the future, redraw the economy of the city around changing technology, but also put us back in touch with our history and traditions, learning from them.'

ALESSANDRO: 'If only we could grasp this emergency as an opportunity to break the deadlock that's kept us prisoners till now, much more than this damned Covid19! Not to mention the rivalries that have prevailed between the old city and the mainland, between the citizens of Venice and Mestre; an opportunity to highlight what unites us rather than what divides us. We are like a complex organism that can only gain from complexity, if we only knew how to value both sides.'

LUCIA: 'Gosh, this old minefield… after five, I repeat *five*, separate referenda on the separation of Venice from Mestre,[9] that have all left things as is… Anyway, this is all boring, can we change the subject? Olga, for example, you haven't told us anything about you? How are you?'

OLGA: 'I should have interjected on the agenda point entitled "Tourism in Venice". But I couldn't be bothered.'

LUCIA: 'Of course, dear, how's the B&B?'

OLGA: 'How do you think? Since I was fired, my only way of surviving was renting out my grandma's little apartment at the Fondamente Nuove.'

MARIO: 'I do remember that pretty furniture shop in Campo Santa Marina, it's a pity they closed down.'

OLGA: 'That two-room apartment was a godsend, at least I was scraping a living together. But now… I'm thinking of renting it on longer-term leases, maybe to students, if lectures ever resume. I would lose out a lot, but at least I'd earn something. Who's going to hire an interior design architect in this climate? Setting up a business at my age and with my scarce finances is out of the question. And it goes without saying there's no support from my ex, you know that I gave up fighting with him. It's easy for you to criticise those who live on tourism, but for me there's no other choice right now.'

MARIO: 'No one's criticising you, honey, we perfectly understand your situation. It's not like you're one of those real estate sharks, we know that.'

Time passes, from one conversation to another, bottles are emptied and others opened, food is devoured, dessert and homemade biscuits appear. It's a pity not being able to eat the food the others have prepared, to share in their delicacies, as well as their conversations, but one has to make the best out of things, waiting for the opportunity to meet again and to decide on a joint menu made up of everyone's specialities, as they had done before on such unforgettable occasions. Mario with his octopus and potato salad, Lucia with her bigoli in salsa,[10] Riccardo with his legendary Venetian style liver,[11] Olga with her bovoleti,[12] Angela with her inescapable guacamole (it's the only thing she makes, but everyone loves it), Elsa with her sangria, Vera with her jam tart.

Paolo was quietly hoping that, in all the chaos, Lucia would forget to keep track of time, but knowing her for as long as he had, he couldn't imagine she would.

And so, a few minutes before half-past three, when some were already starting to feel like a nap, aided by the abundance of the libations, Lucia clinks on a glass with a fork to get everyone's attention.

LUCIA: 'Listen up, please! The clock is about to strike 3:30 on this 25th of April, Liberation Day! Are you ready, comrades?'

PAOLO: 'Oh gosh, Lucia, do we really have to do this?'

LUCIA: 'Hang on a sec, I'm just logging into Facebook, and setting up the livestream. Are you ready? I really care about this. All over Italy at the same time everyone will sing "Bella Ciao", and we must do the same. And in a way, are we not all resisting against an invader these days?'

ALL: 'Una mattina mi son svegliato,
oh bella, ciao! bella, ciao! bella, ciao, ciao, ciao!
Una mattina mi son svegliato
e ho trovato l'invasor.

O partigiano, portami via,
o bella, ciao! bella, ciao! bella, ciao, ciao, ciao!
O partigiano, portami via,
ché mi sento di morir.

E se io muoio da partigiano,
o bella, ciao! bella, ciao! bella, ciao, ciao, ciao!
E se io muoio da partigiano,
tu mi devi seppellir...'[13]

PAOLO: 'You're right guys, the invader and all that. But I, for one, am not looking forward to die, that's clear isn't it?'

LUCIA: 'Paolo, you always have to spoil everything! Anyway, you all look quite worn out after these libations. We should probably say goodbye; the time might be at hand for the postprandial nap. What do you say, shall we arrange to meet again on May Day? Maybe in the evening, next time?'

MARIO: 'Sure, just don't force me to sing "The Internationale" or "Bandiera Rossa"!'

LUCIA: 'Ah, Et tu... always ganging up with your mate. Fine, I promise. Next time no singing.'

One by one, on the screens of each guest's laptop, tablet or mobile, the smiling faces of the brigade start to disappear, but not till everyone has waved their hands in front of the webcam in excessive gestures, throwing kisses, because sometimes, while waiting who knows how long for hugs, words are not enough.

Before going back inside, Paolo and Lucia stop for a moment and lean against the wooden balustrade, to look at the Fondamenta dei Cereri beneath them, silent and deserted, lit by a hot sun that tinges every roof as far as the eye can see, both of them lost in their own thoughts. They turn their eyes towards the campanile of Carmini and, further down, to the one in Santa Margherita. They want to capture this Venice all for themselves as they stand there, which resounds only with the cries of seagulls, the cooing of pigeons and their own footsteps, on the rare occasions they stretch their legs, within the 200-metre radius specified by the government's lockdown measures. Deep down, they desperately hope this situation will offer an occasion to rethink the future of the city. True, the emergency has shown that without tourism Venice dies, but it was dying slowly anyway, invaded by uncontrollable mobs, disrespectful of the narrow, quiet spaces that make the city unique. A solution has to be found, to make Venice an urban reality built for its citizens, not just a big funfair. Neither of them has an answer ready, but they both know there's a need to start working on one right away, everyone together, even if that means giving up the old easy-money, rip-off economy.

Sandra, in turn, looks out the bedroom window of her third-floor apartment in Castello (the dishes can wait). She thinks she will never get used to such magnificence, and Catullo's verse comes back to her. *Odi et amo. Quare id faciam, fortasse requiris. / Nescio, sed fieri sentio et excrucior.*[14] And she thinks that, before this terrible pandemic, there were days when she cursed this city. Its beauty, so extraordinary and unique, had made it arrogant and unbearable, to the point where she couldn't enjoy it. Its slowness was so annoying it burdened her with a tense, explosive, aggressiveness, that often scared her.

This was because Venice tested her, often, with its high tides, its fogs, its never-ending transport strikes. You can't just get in the car here, Sandra thinks, the way you can in the other cities. You have to plan ahead here, if you want to hit the road; and it's even worse if you work on the mainland and live in the old city or vice versa.

To Sandra, it feels like Venice has asked her for unconditional love throughout her life, a love that she hasn't always been willing to give. It asked for her generosity, or rather expected it, because it is an expensive city, a city that charges a lot, not just financially. Venice demands a lot of you. It requires infinite patience, unlimited devotion, if you want to really love it. It demands a lot because it thinks it has a lot to give. Which is often the case.

But Sandra also knows there are days when she truly adores the city. Sometimes, back in the 'normal' times, she would walk out the main door of her museum, in the evening, in Piazza San Marco, and stop for a moment to take in the square people often called (with morose rhetoric) 'the drawing room of Europe' only to find herself full of wonder, then as always, at the reflection of the street lights on the masegni, at the echo of footsteps in the silence, and at the space suddenly vacated by the daily crowds now returned to the beaches or the cabins of cruise ships moored in the port, leaving it once more, just for a short while, alone with her. She imagines that Venice is now finally freed for real, though who knows for how long, but the idea isn't a comforting one; on the contrary, it fills her with anxiety. And this discrepancy doesn't make her feel good.

Moreover, Sandra thinks, there have been days when she couldn't deny being crazy in love with it. She would go to admire it all, with Mario, on the terrace of the Molino Stucky (now a Hilton hotel; nearly all the most beautiful places of Venice have been sacrificed to tourism – luxury tourism mostly – though who's to say what would happen now). They would wait for the twilight to be dazzled by Giudecca's gold, that particular nuance the sunset gives to buildings, rooftops, water. They would wait to be possessed by that extraordinary light that can be found in Canaletto's views, always the same. After all, this is a city that arouses conflicting feelings (not always politically correct) towards those who live here. Even Sandra wished sometimes that she didn't have to share it with anyone. She dreamed of walking along deserted streets, without bumping into a soul along the way, without the need to force her way through parties of cruisers that choked it all year round. But now that this dream, or should it be nightmare, had come true, she finds herself wishing, instead, to be stopped in the street by friends for a chat, just like in any town square. Because in Venice, the few people left all know each other and when they meet they swap stories and tittle-tattle just as all people did, pleasantly, in every town square.

Sandra thinks that in normal times she would have loved to smile at the city, instead of scowl at it all the time; she would have loved to appreciate it, cheerfully, instead of almost always feeling annoyed, disappointed, or resentful towards it. The way you would a love that betrayed you. For Venice prefers someone else. Venice has not loved its citizens for a long time, Sandra thinks but then realises its citizens have also not really loved it in return, given how they've treated it and the choices they've made. But now. Now. Now... Sandra thinks we shall not miss this opportunity to change, change for real. And with these thoughts in her mind, she lays down beside Mario, who is already sleeping soundly.

Notes

1. The 25th of April in Venice is not only the Liberation Day from fascism, but also the day of Saint Mark, the patron of the city. On this day there's a very heartfelt tradition: men give their partners a red rosebud, as a token of love.

2. A kind of finger food eaten in typical Venetian 'bacari', or taverns.

3. Fried sardines with sweet-and-sour onions, a typical Venetian appetiser.

4. In Spanish: *The romanticisation of quarantine is a class privilege!*

5. In Venetian dialect: grocer, grocery store.

6. A 'hanging grocery' is when you pay for something you don't take home with you, but you leave for those who can't afford to shop.

7. On 15th of May 2020, the last of many similar incidents happened: a fire in the 3V Sigma factory in via Malcontenta, in the Porto Marghera area, risked becoming an environmental disaster of much larger proportions.

8. A kind of classification adopted by the Italian National Statistical Institute for national statistical surveys of an economic nature. It stands for Attività Economiche activities.

9. The 1st of December 2019 saw the fifth Regional Referendum on 'Bill No. 8' based on a popular initiative concerning the 'splitting of the municipality of Venice into two autonomous municipalities: one of Venice and one of Mestre,' which failed due to not being quorate.

10. Pasta with anchovies and sometimes also sardines.

11. Venetian liver is the most famous meat dish in the Venetian cuisine; cooked in a pan with plenty of onion, and a handful of pine nuts and raisins.

12. Terrestrial snails that can be collected near the shoreline between April and October, boiled and seasoned with oil and garlic.

13.

One morning I awakened,
oh bella ciao, bella ciao, bella ciao, ciao, ciao! (Goodbye
beautiful)
One morning I awakened
And I found the invader.

Oh partisan carry me away,
oh bella ciao, bella ciao, bella ciao, ciao, ciao
oh partisan carry me away
Because I feel death approaching.

And if I die as a partisan,
oh bella ciao, bella ciao, bella ciao, ciao, ciao
and if I die as a partisan
then you must bury me.

14. 'I hate and I love. You ask me why I do this; I do not know,
but I feel it and it torments me.'

About the Authors

Elisabetta Baldisserotto is a psychoanalyst and writer, living and working in Venice. In addition to numerous articles in specialist magazines, her non-fiction publications include the monographs *Leggere i sentimenti. Un percorso psicologico e letterario* (Read the Feelings: A Psychological and Literary Journey, Moretti & Vitali, 2011), *Figure della passione. Tra psicoanalisi e letteratura* (Figures of Passion: Between Psychoanalysis and Literature, Vivarium, 2014) and *Francesco Baldisserotto. Storia di un patriota veneziano* (Francesco Baldisserotto: Story of an Italian Patriot, Supernova, 2020). She also edited *Diario Analitico. Il mio percorso terapeutico* (An Analytical Diary: My Therapeutic Journey, Vivarium, 2017). Her short fiction includes 'Un caso umano' ('A Human Case' in *Ten Small Ignobles*, edited by B. Graziani, Piazza, 2013). Her short story 'Carmen' (collected in *Ritratti di donne* (Women's Portraits, Terra d'ulivi edizioni, 2020) was winner of the 2002 Pordenonelegge Critics' Prize. She has also published the novels *Morire non è niente* (Dying is Nothing, Cleup, 2015), *Beyond the Water* (Cleup, 2017), awarded the 2018 Giallo Indipendente Award and *Gli occhiali di Hemingway* (Hemingway's Glasses, Cleup, 2019).

Gianfranco Bettin (born in Venice, 1955) is an Italian sociologist, writer and long-time leader of the Greens in Veneto. During his long political career, he was a member of the Italian Parliament (1992–1994), deputy mayor of Venice for Mestre (1995–2005) and member of the Regional Council of Veneto (2000–2010), and is known for his support of

Gianfranco Fini's proposal to give the right to vote to migrants in general elections, and full citizenship rights to migrants in his region. He is the author of eighteen books, including *Cracking* (Mondadori, 2019) and *Qualcosa che brucia* (Something Burning, Garzanti, 1989), a novel exploring working-class Venice.

Annalisa Bruni is a Venetian writer. She has published four collections of short stories: *Storie di libridine* (Edizioni della laguna, 2002), finalist at the 2003 Settembrini-Regione Veneto Prize; *Altri squilibri* (Other Imbalances, Helvetia Edizioni, 2005); *Della felicità donnesca e altri racconti* (Of Female Happiness and Other Stories, Nova Charta, 2008); and *Tipi da non frequentare* (Guys Not to Hang out With, Cleup, 2013), *Tipe da frequentare (ma per quanto?)* (Women to Hang out With – But for How Long?, Cleup, 2016), *Anch'io mi ricordo. Tra Venezia, Mestre e dintorni* (I Remember Too: Venice, Mestre and Around, Cleup, 2019), *Langenwang, ovvero il disastro della puntualità* (Langenwang, or the Disaster of Punctuality, with Stefano Pittarello, Cleup, 2015), *Skyline* (Cleup, 2020). She has also written radio plays broadcast by RAI, Italian Swiss Radio, Croatian National Radio and Czech Radio, and has taught creative writing since 1998.

Michele Catozzi was born in Mestre, Venice in 1960 and has lived for many years in Veneto, where he worked in publishing and journalism. He has been editor in chief of the magazine *Auto d'Epoca* for 25 years, and has been writing short fiction since 1999. His first novel was *Il mistero dell'isola di Candia* (The Mystery of the Island of Candia, GeMS, 2011). Several of his short stories have been published in anthologies and magazines. In 2014 he won the Io Scrittore literary prize for *Acqua Morta* (Dead Water, TEA, 2015) the first in a series of crime novels featuring Inspector Nicola Aldani, a series that has since included *Laguna Nera* (Black Lagoon, TEA, 2017), *Marea Tossica* (Toxic Tide, TEA, 2019) and *Muro di Nebbia* (Wall of Fog, TEA, 2021). Inspector Aldani's investigations are often inspired by real-life events and are interwoven with the city's current problems.

Cristiano Dorigo has worked as a social worker for more than 25 years. He is the co-author of four books and two of his short stories have featured in anthologies published by Marsilio, Einaudi and Prospero. His short stories and texts have been published in Italian and US magazines, newspapers and blogs. He is co-creator and co-writer of the award-winning short film *El mostro* (The Monster, Studio Liz, 2015), and co-curator with Elisabetta Tiveron of *Porto Marghera: cento anni di storie* (Porto Marghera: A Hundred Years of Stories, Helvetia editore, 2017), La *Venezia che vorrei: parole e pratiche per una città felice* (The Venice I Would Like: Words and Practices for a Happy City, Helvetia editrice, 2018) and *Lettere da nordest* (Letters from the North East, Helvetia editrice, 2019).

Roberto Ferrucci (born in Venice, 1960) made his debut in 1993 with the novel *Terra Rossa* (Transeuropa Edizioni), which was followed in 1999 by *Giocando a pallone sull'acqua* (Playing Ball on the Water, Marsilio Editori), *Andate e ritorni* (Roundtrips in the North East, Amos edizioni) in 2003, *Cosa Cambia* (What is Changing, Marsilio) in 2007 and *Sentimenti sovversivi* (Subversive Sentiments, Isbn edizioni) in 2011. He has worked as a journalist, a filmmaker, an editor (for Antiga Edizioni) and is the Italian translator of Jean-Philippe Toussaint and Patrick Deville. Since 2002, he has taught creative writing at the University of Padua, and with Tiziano Scarpa currently co-hosts a writing workshop at the Ca' Foscari University of Venice.

Ginevra Lamberti was born in 1985 and lives in Venice. Her first novel, *La Questione più che altro*, (The Question, More than Anything Else) was published in 2015 by Nottotempo, and translated into French with the title *Avant tut, se poser les bonnes questions* (Le serpent à plumes, 2017) and *Perché comincio dalla fine* (*Why I Begin at the End*, Marsilio, 2019) also published by the Brazilian publisher Âyiné. Her short story 'Carnival' has been translated into German for the anthology *Venedig* (Wagenbach, 2017).

Samantha Lenarda graduated in Literature and Philosophy, specialising in the study of language and dialects, with particular regard to Venetian. She is a short story writer, and has also written several volumes on the Venetian dialect together with Gianfranco Siega and Michela Brugnera: *Fiabe da collezione in dialetto con versione italiana*, (A Collection of Tales, libreria editrice Filippi, 2009), *Dizionario del lessico veneto etimologicamente e curiosamente commentato* (Dictionary of the Venetian Lexicon Etymologically and Curiously Annotated, Finegil Editoriale, 2009), *Il dialetto perduto* (The Lost Dialect, Editoria Universitaria, 2007). Her work is also published on the website, VEV: *Vocabolario storico-etimologico del veneziano* (Historical-Etymological Vocabulary of the Venetian Dialect – http://vev.ovi.cnr.it).

Marilia Mazzeo was born in Ravenna, and has lived in Venice for many years. After studying architecture, she decided to change course and devote herself to writing. She has published one collection of short stories, *Acqua alta* (High Tide, Theoria, 1997), three novels – *Parigi di periferia* (Paris of the Suburbs, EL, 1998), *La ballata degli invisibili*, (The Ballad of the Invisible, Frassinelli, 1999) and *Non troverai altro luogo* (You Won't Find Any Other Place, Frassinelli, 2017) – as well as numerous short stories, some of which have been translated into English, German and French, for anthologies, newspapers and magazines. The diary *Venezia e io* (Venice and I) will be published in 2021 by Helvetia Editrice.

Enrico Palandri (born in Venice, 1956) is an Italian academic, writer, essayist, poet and translator. His early books, *Boccalone* (Edizioni L'Erba Voglio, 1979) and *Le Pietre e il sale* (Ages Apart, Garzanti, 1986) explore the Italian political climate of the 1970s. After his third novel (*Le vie del ritorno*, 1990, translated in German, French and English as *The Way Back*, 1993), Palandri explored storytelling in an unrealistic, fantastic mode (*Allegro fantastico*, 1993). Other novels are, *Le colpevoli ambiguità di Herbert Markus*, (The Guilty Ambiguities of Herbert Markus, Bompiani, 1997), *Angela prende il volo*, (Angela Flies Off, Feltrinelli, 2000), *L'altra sera* (The Other Evening, Feltrinelli 2003), and *I fratelli minori* (Younger Brothers, Bompiani, 2010). The six novels between 1986 and 2010 were woven into a newly written single narrative as *Le condizioni atmosferiche* (Atmospheric Conditions, Bompiani, 2020). Palandri's latest novel was published in 2017, *L'inventore di se stesso* (The Inventor of Himself, Bompiani); it explores some features of the history of Venice through a redefinition of a father and son relationship. He is also a published poet, journalist and radio broadcaster.

About the Translators

Orsola Casagrande is a journalist and filmmaker based variously between Venice, the Basque Country and Havana. As a journalist, she worked for 25 years for the Italian daily newspaper *Il manifesto*, and is currently co-editor of the web magazine *Global Rights*. She writes regularly for Spanish, Catalan and Basque newspapers. While living in Cuba, she covered the Colombia peace process. She has translated numerous books, including *The Second Prison* by Ronan Bennett (Gamberetti, 2004) and *The Fountain at the Centre of the World* by Robert Newman (Giunti, 2008) as well as written her own books: *Tower Colliery* (Odradek 2004) and *Berxwedan* (Punto Rosso 2008). She is the editor and co-translator of Comma's *The Book of Havana,* and co-editor of *The American Way: Stories of Invasion* (with Ra Page) and *Kurdistan + 100* (with Mustafa Gundogdu), both forthcoming from Comma.

Caterina Dell'Olivo is a Venetian translator and proofreader. After graduating from Ca' Foscari University, she received a Masters degree in Translation in Turin, where she is now based. She has collaborated with several publishing houses, including UTET De Agostini (*The Nutshell Technique*), Newton Compton (*Royals, Summer at the Skylark Farm*) and Rizzoli, both translating and proofreading.

The Book of Birmingham, Edited by Khavita Bhanot

The Book of Cairo, Edited by Raph Cormack

The Book of Dhaka, Edited by Arunava Sinha & Pushpita Alam

The Book of Gaza, Edited by Atef Abu Saif

The Book of Havana, Edited by Orsola Casagrande

The Book of Tehran, Edited by Fereshteh Ahmadi

The Book of Istanbul, Edited by Jim Hinks & Gul Turner

The Book of Jakarta, Edited by Maesy Ang
& Teddy W. Kusuma

The Book of Khartoum, Edited by Raph Cormack
& Max Shmookler

The Book of Leeds, Edited by Tom Palmer & Maria Crossan

The Book of Liverpool, Edited by Maria Crossan & Eleanor Rees

The Book of Newcastle, Edited by Angela Readman
& Zoe Turner

The Book of Ramallah, Edited by Maya Abu Al-Hayat

The Book of Riga, Edited by Becca Parkinson
& Eva Eglaja-Kristsone

The Book of Rio, Edited by Toni Marques & Katie Slade

The Book of Shanghai, Edited by Dai Congrong & Jin Li

The Book of Sheffield, Edited by Catherine Taylor

The Book of Tbilisi, Edited by Becca Parkinson & Gvantsa Jobava

The Book of Tokyo, Edited by Jim Hinks, Masashi Matsuie
& Michael Emmerich

The Book of Jakarta

Edited by Maesy Ang & Teddy W. Kusuma

Made up of over 17,000 islands, Indonesia is the fourth most populous country on the planet. It is home to hundreds of different ethnicities and languages, and a cultural identity that is therefore constantly in flux. Like the country as a whole, the capital Jakarta is a multiplicity of irreducible, unpredictable and contradictory perspectives.

From down-and-out philosophers to roadside entertainers, the characters in these stories see Jakarta from all angles. Traversing different neighbourhoods and social strata, their stories capture the energy, aspirations, and ever-changing landscape of what is also the world's fastest-sinking city.

Featuring: utiuts, Sabda Armandio, Hanna Fransisca, Cyntha Hariadi, Afrizal Malna, Dewi Kharisma Michellia, Ratri Ninditya, Yusi Avianto Pareanom, Ben Sohib & Ziggy Zezsyazeoviennazabrizkie

ISBN: 978-1-91269-732-8
£9.99

The Book of Ramallah

Edited by Maya Abu Al-Hayat

Unlike most other Palestinian cities, Ramallah is a relatively new town, a de facto capital of the West Bank allowed to thrive after the Oslo Peace Accords, but just as quickly hemmed in and suffocated by the Occupation as the Accords have failed. Perched along the top of a mountainous ridge, it plays host to many contradictions: traditional Palestinian architecture jostling against aspirational developments and cultural initiatives, a thriving nightlife in one district, with much more conservative, religious attitudes in the next. Most striking however – as these stories show – is the quiet dignity, resilience and humour of its people; citizens who take their lives into their hands every time they travel from one place to the next, who continue to live through countless sieges, and yet still find the time, and resourcefulness, to create.

Featuring: Liana Badr, Ahlam Bsharat, Ameer Hamad, Maya Abu Al-Hayat, Khaled Hourani, Ahmad Jaber, Ziad Khadash, Ibrahim Nasrallah, Anas Abu Rahma, Mahmoud Shukair

ISBN: 978-1-91269-742-7
£9.99

The Book of Shanghai

Edited by Dai Congrong & Jin Li

The characters in this literary exploration of one of the world's biggest cities are all on a mission. Whether it is responding to events around them, or following some impulse of their own, they are defined by their determination – a refusal to lose themselves in a city that might otherwise leave them anonymous, disconnected, alone.

From the neglected mother whose side-hustle in collecting sellable waste becomes an obsession, to the schoolboy determined to end a long-standing feud between his family and another, these characters show a defiance that reminds us why Shanghai – despite its hurtling economic growth –remains an epicentre for individual creativity.

Featuring: Wang Anyi, Xiao Bai, Shen Dacheng, Chen Danyan, Cai Jun, Chen Qiufan, Xia Shang, Teng Xiaolan, Fu Yuehui & Wang Zhanhei

ISBN: 978-1-91269-727-4
£9.99